Be sure to check out these other thrilling titles in our Grave Marker line, available digitally for your Kindle.

Nikolis Cole: The Low-rise Saint by Richard Black
Rock, Paper, Scissors by Sebastian Bendix
Coattails by Joshua Rex
Tolerance by Hal Bodner
Shriek of the Harpy by Sebastian Bendix
The One Who Lies Next to You by Russell Coy
Full Moon in the West by Dominic Stabile
Bottled Spirits by Adrian Ludens
The Dance by S.L. Williams
The Freaks Come Out at Night by Joseph Rubas
The First Suitor by A.P. Sessler
Vampire Worms by Neil Davies

Grave Markers
Volume 5

W.C. Jones, A.P. Sessler,

and Andrew Richardson

A
Grinning Skull Press
Publication

PO Box 67
Bridgewater, MA 02324

CONTENTS

A WORD ABOUT GRAVE MARKERS

I promise to keep this short so you can get on to reading the tales collected in this volume. Folks often ask about Grave Markers and what they are. Grave Markers are, in a word, novelettes. They are stories too long to be included in anthologies (which usually average 5,000 to 7,000 words) but not quite long enough to be published on their own as stand-alone novellas. They are published individually in digital formats, and then later compiled into a print collection. The reason why we started this line is we often heard authors commenting that there wasn't a market for those "in-between" length stories and we wanted to give them an outlet for such pieces. And that about sums it up. Told you I'd keep it short. Now, without further ado, I present to you the premier collection of Grave Markers. Enjoy!

Michael J. Evans
Grinning Skull Press

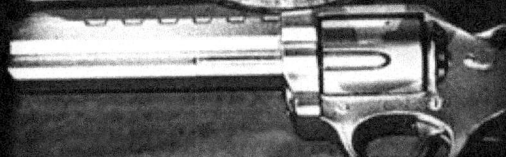

W.C. JONES

THE SOURCE

Dedication

For my son, Christopher, who fuels my inspiration,

and

For my wife, Wendy, the gentlest and harshest critic I have ever met.

Chapter One

Now before you go and pass judgment on me, you have to know why I did what I did. The highway to Hell is paved with good intentions as they say. That's true for most bad ideas, but not all. If you don't believe me, go pick up a copy of Mary Shelley's *Frankenstein*. The protagonist of that story had very good intentions indeed. He wanted to defeat death itself by creating life. Sounds noble, doesn't it?

Well, when he tried to go through with this plan, all he succeeded in doing was creating an immortal monster that killed everyone who ever meant anything to him. So much for good intentions, right?

Now, I'm not trying to compare myself to that story's crazy doctor. At least not intentionally. You see, I never wanted to prevent anything or change some cataclysmic truth about life. I'm not a modern day Plato or Socrates, and I never tried to be.

No, the highway that led to my own hell started when I was just a little boy. Kids are very impressionable, you know. They believe the world is practically flawless until something happens to destroy this image they have. Well, mine came when I was nine; I had just watched a very interesting news story, one that sparked my curiosity enough to ask a question that would change my life forever.

Chapter Two

"Dad, why do bad things happen?"

The question must have caught my father off guard because he spent a few moments rubbing a calloused hand through his graying beard before responding.

"That's a question for the man upstairs."

We were sitting out on the porch during a blistering summer day.

"So, you think God knows?"

"He must, considering he allows it to exist in the first place." Dad roughed up my hair with fingers that had cracked and bled for over a decade picking up bricks and blocks. Sometimes his touch felt weird, like having a piece of sandpaper sliding across the top of my head.

"If He doesn't, then who would?"

Dad frowned and several wrinkles appeared around his eyes. He took his hand away and sighed. "Why are you so interested to know?"

"I saw it on the news," I said. "Some lady took her new puppies and stuck them in a microwave!"

"Why would she do that?"

"She said she just felt like it."

"She's a terrible person, I must say."

"Yeah," I said, my eyes searching his.

He remained silent for a few moments, then calmly stood up and wiped his boots off near the front door before opening it and going inside. I felt betrayed, like he knew the answer I wanted but refused to tell me. It was like being excluded from a secret clubhouse, one I'd worked hard to join, just to be told "thanks, but no thanks."

Even though I asked him the same question many times growing up, his answer never changed. He would just get frustrated after a while and tell me to stop obsessing over it.

Mom was the same way. She would calmly listen to my questions, especially those based on other news stories or even the tales being passed around at school. A boy with short, brown hair and a pudgy face named Tommy told me how his uncle beat his wife with a Louisville Slugger. She ended up in a wheelchair, and he currently stayed at the prison a few towns away. Though he would probably never get out, it didn't seem enough to me, especially when Tommy described how his aunt could only move her neck and took her food through a tube.

Mom made me promise to stay away from him when I told her the story, stating that he would be a bad influence on me. I told her I would, but he and I continued to talk until he moved a few years later.

School revealed some truly shocking things, most of them in places I would have never thought to look. In my history class with Mrs. Shedd, a short, plumpish woman who looked a hundred years old, we learned about a man named Adolf Hitler. He smiled up at me from the page, his arm raised in a weird salute. Though the picture was in black and white, I thought his clothes looked nice, professional even. He looked like some-one getting ready to enjoy a fun day in the park, only in front of a lot of similarly dressed people, all of which held their arms up in the same salute. There was a slight mist obscuring the picture, but I figured the old-timey cameras weren't as good as the more modern ones. Well, this smiling man with the tiny mustache had made a hobby out of torturing and killing mil-lions of Jewish people. Mrs. Shedd was a Jew herself, and she held nothing back when she discussed the various methods this man employed to get what he wanted—which just happened to be the systematic genocide of an entire race of people.

Like the woman who microwaved her puppies, he did it because he felt like it.

Chapter Three

By the time I graduated high school, my girlfriend, Tracy, sprung the news that my days of freedom were coming to an end. The pregnancy came as a shock to both of us because we always used protection. I chalked it up to God having a strange sense of humor.

We were both working at the time, but despite being unmarried, we decided the best course of action was to move in together. This proved much more difficult than we thought. For starters, apartments were extremely expensive in town, especially the two-bedroom ones we felt we'd need when the baby arrived. Tracy was working down at the local grill, and I was delivering pizzas five days a week.

Needless to say, our finances weren't cutting it. We ended up moving into a single-bedroom in a semi-shady part of town. Tracy hated it, but this was the best we could do with what we had.

"What am I going to do when some crackhead decides to break in while you're working a late shift?"

She was standing next to me as I pulled on my work boots. I took a moment to think about the question, knowing that any answer I gave wouldn't cut it.

"You still have that pistol your father gave you?"

"Yes, but I don't even know how to shoot it."

She stepped closer and put a hand on my shoulder; her long, dirty blonde hair cascaded down her shoulders, and the purple tank top she had on revealed enough of her lovely figure that I wished I didn't have to go to work.

I finished tying my boot and turned to face her. Her expression was soft, yet held a pinch of real concern.

"Honey, you are going to be fine."

"But…how do you know?"

"I just do." I reached down and picked up the ball cap with the fading *Randy's Pizza* logo on it. The feel of it was still strange, more of an unwelcomed pest than a mainstay.

Tracy planted one on my lips. "You be careful," she said as she pulled back. "For both of us." She patted her belly, and even though she was still not showing any weight gain, I placed my hand over hers.

"Will do."

I had no clue these would be the last words I ever spoke to her, and that I would never see my future baby in even its early stages. The bullets that took her and our still-unnamed child came not from someone trying to break in, but from a single dark car that sprayed several houses on the block. Tracy must have been sitting in her reading chair when the gunfire tore through the wall because her body was found still sitting up, her eyes wide as if in shock, an open book lying face down on the floor in front of her.

She wasn't the only victim either; an older black neighbor and two teenagers were also found riddled. The police decided it was some kind of gang hit—which is entirely plausible—but no one recognized the vehicle, and it was too dark to see the plate number.

I spat in my boss's face and cursed before quitting my job after he tried to force me back to work less than two days after Tracy's funeral. Beer and whiskey became my two best friends for a while. They burned my throat and made the room spin so badly I would wake up on the floor of the motel room the police put me in during the investigation, the same one that I still hadn't left yet.

I think I probably would have been found by the maid, dead from alcohol poisoning, if one of my old friends from high school, Fred Barden, hadn't shown up one day. He was dressed in a flannel shirt, red with white stripes, and was trying his best to look cheerful.

"Well, I'll be," I said, "if it isn't Bait himself."

Bait was a nickname the guys and I bestowed on him when we first entered ninth grade. See, he was overweight back then, and a lot of the jocks used to seek him out like a shark does a bleeding fish. They would tear into him with slaps to the back of the head and some of the worst insults I'd ever heard before. They were always prowling the hallways looking for him, so when my friends and I hung around him, we became their targets as well. Thus, we called him Bait because he always brought trouble to himself and to us.

It had been about three weeks since I quit my job, and my parents had made it very clear that they were tired of lending me money. They offered to clean up my old bedroom and have me stay with them, but that was completely out of the question as far as I was concerned. I didn't feel like getting any more lectures.

Fred forced a smile and pushed his glasses up. "How have you been, man?"

"I'm doing fine." I had answered the door in a dirty wife beater and a pair of briefs. To his credit, however, Fred never mentioned this fact.

"Well, that's good. I mean, given the circumstances and all."

A picture of Tracy formed in my thoughts, and a pang of sadness tried to blow a hole in the wall I'd built to contain it.

"Thanks for that…" I said, still forcing the wall to continue standing, barely succeeding. "…really."

"Can I come in? Or is now a bad time?"

I became aware of what I looked like and my face grew warm. "Actually, give me a second to throw something else on."

I closed the door and pulled a semi-dirty pair of shorts from the pile of laundry I still hadn't taken to the laundromat a few blocks away. The stench was noticeable but faint, good enough for a quick visit. Fred was standing next to the railing by the stairs when I came out. My room was on the second floor, and the landing overlooked a grassy field that led to a thick patch of forest. As I stepped up to him, the small group of rabbits he'd been watching suddenly scattered and he turned around.

"That's way better man."

I managed a weak laugh. "In looks maybe, but the stench, whew! Remind me never to wait 'til the end of the week to do laundry ever again!"

Fred nodded and then crossed his arms. He slimmed down in eleventh grade and began lifting weights his senior year. He was by no means a bodybuilder, but had gained a fair bit of muscle that made me want to get back into a gym at the earliest opportunity.

"So," he said, a grin forming on his face. "I heard you don't have a job right now."

"You heard right. My wallet is full of cobwebs, and thanks to cursing out big John, I'll bet he's already called every business in town to warn them about me."

His grin widened, and for a moment he reminded me of the same jocks that used to pick on him, minus the glasses. "Well, I've got a solution for you. One I think you'll like."

"I'm all ears."

"The trucking company that hired me has recently lost several employees and is willing to hire just about anyone at this point. So—"

"You're kidding, right?"

"Nope. I think this would be good for you, man. The pay's not bad either."

"Don't you have to be qualified for that?" I threw up my hands. "I can barely drive a standard, let alone a semi!"

Fred chuckled and uncrossed his arms. "That's not a problem. Heck, I was never that good at driving that old Pontiac of mine, and I still managed."

"That's because you're weird and seem to be good at everything you do."

"Look, cut the crap." Fred's smile vanished, and he looked even more like the ones who used to torment him. "The company will pay for your training just like they did mine. I mean, come on, Josh, you can't keep going on like this—"

"Just stop right there before you go any further." I could feel heat rising, getting ready to erupt in a fiery swarm of thrown punches and kicks. Underneath this feeling, however, there was a revelation: He was right, even if he was being a little pushy about it. I desperately needed something better than hanging out with my current best friends, Budweiser and Jim Bean.

"I'm not going to stop and let you destroy yourself, man. You can be mad at me or whatever you want but—"

"Okay, I'll do it."

"—you know I'm—what?"

"I said I'll do it. I'll apply for the position. Where can I get an application, and who do I have to call to set up the training?"

"Already done. I told my boss you'd start training tomorrow." Fred's grin was back, his sign of victory. "So get your smelly clothes together and check out. You can crash at my place until you find an apartment."

"Nah, I'll just be your roommate and hog all the water and food."

"Ha ha, very funny."

I smiled, and for the first time in a long while, it was genuine.

Chapter Four

Training wasn't as bad as I thought it would be. Growing up, I always believed the bigger something was, the harder it was to control, but when I got behind the wheel of a semi for the first time, it pretty much drove itself.

My instructor was an older gentleman named Charles. He had a wide frame and an infectious smile. By the time the training ended two weeks later, I knew all about his three failed marriages, the two daughters he only saw during the holidays, and his worries and concerns about his German Shepherd, Doug.

Once I received my certification, Fred offered to partner drive with me. This sounded good on paper, but I wanted to spend some time by myself, so I politely declined.

"Okay, whatever, man, just thought it would be a good idea," he said, then strolled quickly out of the break room and left me to finish a particularly bland ham sandwich with mustard.

I sat there and looked around at all the various safety posters, the occasional pin-up from a *Hustler* magazine, and several tables with their chairs pulled out.

I had been doing a lot of thinking, mostly about Tracy. The police still hadn't made any arrests, and without any eyewitnesses coming forth, they probably never would. I wondered how our lives would have been with a new baby, the sleepless nights. I had secretly looked forward to fixing bottles in the wee hours of the morning and then taking my son (or would it have been a girl?) into my arms and poking that little rubber nipple between those tiny pink gums. I can honestly say I am a very tough guy when it comes to my emotions, but every time I thought about holding my child in my arms, then realizing that it would never happen, it brought me to my knees with the force of the sobs that escaped my trembling lips.

It didn't take long, however, before the sadness became rage. It wasn't fair that I would never get to hold the baby that died the moment Tracy's life ended; it wasn't fair that the ones responsible for such evil would never be brought to justice. What made them do what they did? What force would the maker of the universe allow to create such horror and mayhem in the lives of his children?

Where did evil itself come from?

The obvious answer was from other people, but the fact that one could choose whether to shoot a man for the two dollars in his wallet or simply walk away rendered that response too simple.

There had to be something more.

Yes, one could choose to be evil, but that all came from making a decision on the inside. There was always that inner voice, the one saying it's alright to rob the local Kroger's, and that if someone gets shot, it's okay because rent is due tomorrow. Still, where did this voice come from? Was it really just mental hocus-pocus?

I took another bite of my sandwich and contemplated throwing the rest away. Then a thought occurred to me: wouldn't that action alone be somewhat evil? By throwing away my food, I would take away any chance to give it to someone who might need it.

I chewed another bite, the contents doing nothing to satisfy my hunger, and tossed the rest of it in the wastebasket near the door. Then I walked out and couldn't keep from smiling.

Chapter Five

After picking up a load from Dallas, I had to bring it to Little Rock, Arkansas. The freeways coming out of Texas were always jammed, and I cursed at every vehicle, be it a car, truck, station wagon, Honda, or Ford. People today just don't know how to use turn signals and brake lights.

A storm raged overhead, the constant spatter of rain making it harder and harder to see the lines on the road. It didn't help that the windshield wiper on the left side only worked when it wanted to. It would dart forward and backward like clockwork for a few moments, then it would stop for twenty seconds, letting a fine sheet of water blur half my field of vision, then start back up only to die again.

I ended up almost pushing a smaller Volvo into the guardrail due to concentrating too much on the wiper blade. I missed him by less than a hair it seemed, and he quickly darted around me blaring his horn a few times. I needed to rest and got off at the next exit. There was a Fill'er Up Quickmart a little after the end of the ramp, and the idea of getting some food and a quick, warm shower made me feel warm and cozy inside. As luck would have it, there was a small diner attached to the edge of the building, and as I pulled in the entrance way, a smile crept across my face.

The rain slacked off a little as I followed a crude set of arrows toward the back of the building where several other semis lay in hiding. No doubt their operators were either snoozing on the pull-out beds or watching a dirty movie they bought on their return trip.

I parked and quickly got out, forgetting the umbrella lying on the passenger's seat. The water hitting me all over sent cool shocks through my body, as if someone was poking me with ice-cold needles all over at once. A flash of lightning brought the world into better focus for a moment, then plunged it back into darkness before the clouds growled another warning.

My shirt had come unbuttoned at some point and flapped wildly around me like wings. The wind tried to push me back every time I took a step forward, but I kept moving toward sanctuary. The building was tall and rectangular, although the roof sloped towards the front. The small diner jutted out of the far left side, and it was there that I spied light streaming through a pair of windows. The neon sign hanging in front glowed with a message I welcomed:

OPEN 24 Hours! SHOWERS AVAILABLE!

I sprinted through the rain, pulling my shirt up over my head to keep from getting completely soaked. When I reached the door, a woman pushed it open for me. She wore a pink uniform with a black apron tied around her waist.

"Hurry up, Hun, or you'll catch your death out there!"

"Thanks," I said as I stepped inside. The sudden warmth wrapped around me with gentle fingers that threatened to send me into a coma the first time I sat down.

"No problem."

I pulled the shirt off my head and straightened it out as much as I could. Water dripped all over and created small puddles at my feet.

"Sorry 'bout the floor."

"Don't worry about that, I'll get a mop to it in just a few moments." She gestured to a long counter surrounded by chairs that were bolted into the floor. "You just have a seat and try to dry off."

I nodded and took her advice.

The bar reminded me of the one in that famous painting *Nighthawks* by an artist whom I'd studied in high school. It stretched out from the wall and snaked its way in a large semi-circle all the way to the other side of the same wall, leaving walking space on the inside for a few waitresses to place orders on the overhead window that connected to the kitchen.

I chose a seat near the right side and plopped my weary bones down. Someone was cooking bacon in the back, and the sizzling and popping of the grease mixed with its irresistible aroma reminded me how hungry I was. The last stop I'd made was a McDonald's in Dallas before picking up the load. That dollar cheeseburger hadn't put a dent in my appetite.

"That smells really good."

The waitress smiled. Here, in the light hanging over the bar, she was quite a looker. Her face was soft, and the dirty blonde hair hanging slightly above her shoulders reminded me of Tracy's.

"Burt's cooking always smells divine, if you ask me," she said.

There was another woman behind the counter; her hands were buried in a sink below my sightline. She looked up only momentarily at my voice but then dropped her head and kept working.

"Tell him to throw on four more slices for me. And some scrambled eggs, if you got'em."

"Sure thing, Hun." The first waitress pulled out a yellow receipt pad and scribbled the order down while I watched. "You want anything else? Maybe some hash browns or something to drink?"

"Is the coffee fresh?"

"It was made an hour ago."

"Sounds good."

She smiled at me, more than a little flirtatious. "I'll be right back with your coffee."

After she disappeared behind a sliding door that led to the kitchen, I turned my head and gazed around the room. For a truck stop to have so many semis parked in the back, there was no one else in the diner besides myself, the waitresses, and their cook, along with one other gentleman that I could barely see.

He was half-hidden in a large booth that could have easily seated ten or more. Without going closer to get a better look, he appeared to be wearing a dark coat with a hood. His face was mostly hidden except for his mouth and nose.

Something bothered me about him instantly, but I couldn't put my finger on it. He looked harmless enough, but his lips constantly moved, as if he was having a conversation with someone sitting next to him.

"Here you go, Hun," said the dirty blonde waitress as she set a steaming cup of black coffee in front of me. "Do you want any creamer?"

I turned my attention back to her, forgetting the strange man in the corner.

"Excuse me?"

"Creamer, Hun, do you want any?"

"Oh, yes, that's fine. Four, if you please."

Her smile lessened, and she leaned down close enough that I could smell faint remnants of tobacco smoke as she spoke.

"Are you okay?"

"Yeah, it's just..." I said, thinking about asking her about the other customer. Was he was a regular? Did he always talk to himself? Instead, I decided to play it cool. "It's been a long day. I guess I'm just exhausted."

She put a hand on my shoulder and rubbed it softly. "I'm not surprised. It's after midnight."

I nodded and thanked her for showing such concern. A few minutes later my food arrived, and I forgot all about the man who was talking to himself. The bacon was soft, yet had a satisfying crunch to it, and the eggs were fluffy and warm. Just like Tracy used to make them. My hunger was stronger than I thought it would be, and once I polished off my plate, I ordered some hash browns to go with it. After the waitress took the first plate and brought the second one, I decided that Tracy's cooking was better.

Tears threatened to spill down my face, but I forced them back in, the effort leaving my face feeling uncomfortably warm.

I raised my hand to signal for the check when the man at the back of the diner stood up, revealing a second figure in the booth that hadn't been there before. It was hazy and featureless, a shadow.

Only it wasn't attached to any owner.

Fear crept into my stomach and rose quickly up my spine as the hooded man stalked towards the front counter. I saw more of his face then; he was young, probably around his late twenties. His eyes shone under the lights, and his expression was grim with its lack of emotion.

He held a small, black pistol in his right hand.

My immediate response was to throw my hands up in surrender. The waitress washing the dishes suddenly dropped the plate she'd been holding, and it smashed on the floor. The sound it made brought the other waitress out, but before she had a chance to ask what happened, the hooded figure brandished the gun out in front of him and aimed at her.

"Oh, God!" she screamed.

The man's voice was poison to the air, and his expression never changed as he spoke. "Give me all the money from the register and the safe."

"Take it easy, fella," I said, my arms still pointed towards the ceiling. "You don't want to do this."

The man turned his attention to me. His glassy eyes bore into mine. A slight scar trailed down his left cheek and continued into his upper lip as if he had taken a razor to the side of his face. Though his appearance was shocking and disturbing in its own right, it wasn't what suddenly closed my mouth and made my eyes go wide with alarm.

It was the shadow.

The same hazy figure I first saw in the booth had followed him. It drifted immediately behind him, and suddenly a section of it enveloped his right shoulder blade like a hand.

"Stay out of this, or I'll put a bullet between your eyes," the man said, his expression never changing.

"*Shoot him if he tries to interfere,*" said a low, threatening voice that hadn't come from him or anyone else standing around.

I watched as the man's eyes twitched, and then the misty figure hovering behind him leaned closer, settled less than an inch from his ear.

"*Think of Carley. You don't want to lose the house to the bank, do you?*"

He shook his head, then he brought the gun on me. "Get on the ground, now!"

I slipped out of the stool and lay face down, put my hands behind my head. The whole time this went on, I wasn't as afraid of getting shot as I was of seeing what the shadow was doing.

The rest of the incident played out fairly quickly, and from what I heard with my face on the floor, the dirty blonde waitress emptied the register and piled the day's earnings into a bag while trying to avoid hysteria. The other waitress was instructed to do as I had done, and I heard her sobbing from behind the counter.

"*What about the cook?*" the voice whispered. "*He could be calling the police.*"

My blood grew cold, and the chill it sent up my spine was enough to send painful bolts down into my thighs. The sheer impossibility of the situation sent my mind racing for something logical to grasp, but there was nothing to find.

"You in the kitchen," the man cried out suddenly. "Get out here, or

I blow a hole in this pretty waitress!"

I heard the whine of the sliding door opening, and then a man's voice, gripped by fear. "Okay, I'm here, don't shoot."

"Get down on the ground—"

"*The main door*," the voice said, its tone sounding almost joyful. "*There's someone coming.*"

I turned my head and was able to see the figure approaching. It was a heavy-set man. He carried an umbrella in his right hand and was walking quickly to get out of the rain. His obliviousness to the danger produced a helpless feeling I never want to experience again.

"*I'll bet he's carrying a gun*," the voice said, its tone growing more alarming than before. "*He's coming to stop you.*"

I was too slow to prevent what happened; the heavy-set man opened the door and took two steps, reached to pull down his umbrella when the pistol went off. The shot caught him right below his left eye, and he staggered back, the umbrella falling from his hand, still open. He then crumpled like a puppet that's had its strings cut.

I don't know what pushed me to grab the gunman's leg and tug it. Maybe it was a sudden surge of adrenaline, but when I did, it sent him falling backward. The gun went off and blew a chunk out of one of the stools. The waitress behind the counter screamed at the same time as her companion. The cook, however, took advantage of my sneak attack and stepped on the man's right hand, pinning the gun to the floor.

He fired two more times, and the bullets created holes in the wall next to the kitchen. Then the cook's foot found his trigger finger and crunched down so hard he couldn't move it anymore.

26

"Get off me you prick!"

The hooded man twisted and brought his other hand over to free himself. The cook was slightly heavier than he was, and the effort proved fruitless as the balding man with the white apron kicked him square on the jaw and forced him to be still.

Adrenaline still coursing through my veins, I quickly got to my feet in case the guy came to and tried anything. He was unconscious and barely breathing. There was a sliver of blood trailing from his bottom lip, but otherwise, he appeared to be unharmed.

The cook looked at me, his eyes wide. Sweat glistened on his slightly pudgy face. "I got this piece of trash," he said. "Go check the guy at the front door!"

I ran to check on the heavy-set man with the umbrella. I didn't have to check his pulse to know he was dead. His eyes were open, his face frozen in a moment of shock.

"He's gone," I called back to the cook.

He cursed loudly, and I turned back around to see him holding the gun on the murderer, his hands shaking. The dirty blonde-haired waitress was busy calling the police, while the other waitress was silent behind the counter. I walked around to check on her and found she had fainted. Her eyes were closed, and only the steady rise and fall of her chest sig-naled that she was still alive.

For the moment, I had forgotten about the shadow and the voice, but that all changed when I focused again on the cook. He was standing over the gunman, the pistol trembling in his hand. The same shadow that had hung around the hooded man now hovered at his side. It appeared slightly larger than before but still retained its humanoid shape.

As I watched, unable to move, it leaned over close enough to whisper in his ear.

"*No one would blame you,*" it said, its voice almost like a hiss. "*He already killed a man. One pull of that trigger would ensure he never does it again.*"

Sweat glistened on the cook's face. I could see the struggle taking place. He was seriously considering pulling the trigger.

"*Just squeeze one off,*" the voice continued. "*Everyone here will claim it was self-defense.*"

"No," I shouted, and he suddenly snapped the gun in my direction. "Don't do it!"

He blinked a few times before lowering it. "I'm sorry, I don't know what came over me." He slowly trained the gun back on the hooded figure.

I didn't offer a response; I was too busy watching the shadow. It floated back a few feet, its head still facing him. Then it turned, and if its shape had had a pair of eyes, they would have focused solely on me.

"My God," I said, bringing my hand to my face.

It turned away and walked—or glided rather—toward the front door. Then it drifted out into the rainy night. Without thinking, I followed it, my legs aching from the sudden pressure exerted on them. I burst through the door, and as the first of many raindrops pelted my face, I scanned the parking lot.

It was gone.

The police arrived and took the gunman away, and after the interview I gave the arresting officer at the scene (I didn't include the shadow part because I didn't want to come off sounding like a lunatic), I went back to my truck to catch a few hours of sleep, deciding to let my boss know that the drop off in Arkansas would be late. I figured he would understand given the circumstances. Try as I might, though, I couldn't sleep.

Chapter Six

When I finished dropping the load at the Little Rock depot, I decided to grab a quick lunch and then call it a day. I figured I'd made a pretty decent paycheck, so I wasn't overly worried about getting started again. I kept thinking about the gunman in the diner. His lifeless expression. And the shadow. The thought of it brought goose-flesh to my arms despite the heat in the break room. I had just polished off another ham sandwich, this one much tastier than the other one before, and I was starting on a small bag of cool ranch Doritos when an older gentlemen wearing a dark jumpsuit walked into the room and sat at a table next to me.

He wore a New York Yankees baseball cap, so I figured he was probably a Yankee himself, maybe born close to Boston or Maine. So I was surprised when he opened his mouth and a thick, southern accent came out.

"You okay there, feller? You lookin' like you've had a good scare."

I chewed and swallowed before responding. "Yeah, I guess I have."

He smiled with a set of yellow teeth stained by coffee and cigarettes that could very well have been dentures.

"Happens to the best of us."

"Not like this," I said.

"Oh?" His eyes seemed to brighten, as if a large syringe full of curiosity was enough to restore lost youth in an aging face. "How so?"

I wanted to tell him everything: the robbery, the shadow, and what it almost did to the cook. Everything.

Yet I couldn't. Instead, I simply kept quiet and piled chips into my mouth. The older man took the hint after a few moments, pulled out a large thermos, and poured a steaming cup of coffee for himself.

After he took a big swig and swallowed it, he looked back at me and frowned. The wrinkles around his eyes told of his years of experience, somewhat harsh judging by the severity of his skin.

"Listen, son," he began, his eyes growing dimmer as he leaned forward to make sure I heard him. "I've been around quite a while, and I've seen some pretty nasty things. Some of 'em still keep me up at night."

I nodded then waited for him to continue.

"Judging from your age and the fact that I've never seen you around here before, I'm guessing you're green around the gills when it comes to a lot of things, and that's okay. Experience is the best teacher, especially for the young tadpoles like yourself." He stopped to take another swig of coffee, swallowed it quickly. "One thing you're going to find out real quick, especially in this business, is how insane the world really is. I mean it's so crazy that not even Mister Freud could have fixed it!"

I didn't really care for being compared to a baby frog, but this conversation was a distraction from my thoughts, so I kept listening.

"It's the truth by gawd," he said, and slammed a fist down on the table. "Take this one, for instance: I was driving a load up to Vegas about fifteen years ago. You know how congested the freeways are? Well, the one leading into Nevada was a never-ending sea of cars that moved a few inches every five minutes or so."

He paused to take another drink. A few beads of sweat gathered on his forehead, but he removed his ball cap, wiped it away with his other hand. "Needless to say, there were a lot of angry drivers."

"I'll bet."

"That's not the best part," he said. "Oh no sir! Right in front of me sat a fancy-looking Chevy Cobalt housing a man in a gray business suit. I didn't really get a look at his face, but I sure heard his horn clear enough. He kept hitting it every fifteen seconds or so, as if he thought the red truck in front of him had no reason not to move."

"So what did the truck driver do?"

"Oh, it wasn't him. No, it was the guy over on the right side of the Chevy. He was riding in a beat-up Pontiac Sun fire, probably an early 90s model by the looks of it, but man, the guy behind the wheel kept looking over at the businessman and shaking his head. I could see his face in the hanging mirror. Kept moving his mouth steadily, almost as if he were talking to himself. Every once in a while he would turn to the passenger's side as if someone was with him."

The color drained from my face, and I could tell he noticed because he stopped talking and stared at me, trying to figure out which part of his story had upset me more.

"Are you sure the guy in the Pontiac was alone? That he didn't have some kind of companion?"

He looked at me in a way that suggested that he was trying to decide if I was some kind of lunatic.

"Yes, I'm sure he didn't. I may be older than you by a few decades, but the last time I checked, I'm not blind."

"Go on," I whispered, a slow feeling of dread inching up my spine. "What happened?"

"Well, I could tell the guy in the Pontiac was getting angry, but when he suddenly got out, I had no clue what was gettin' ready to go down." He took another quick sip, swallowed, and continued. "Poor guy in the Chevy never saw it coming."

"What happened?" I demanded, any patience I had flying out the window.

"He walked behind the Chevy, reached into the back of his jeans, and brought out a revolver. Then he took aim and fired three shots into the back glass."

"Didn't anyone call the cops?"

"Of course they did," he said, raising a hand suddenly then slapping it down on the table again. "I was one of 'em. But that didn't save old businessman, no sir! That first shot exploded the back of his head like a watermelon."

"What did the driver do after killing the guy in the Chevy?"

His eyes grew smaller, more serious. "That's the weirdest part. He simply put the gun back in his jeans and calmly walked back to his vehicle. He was still waiting in the traffic line when the police arrived."

"Did he continue to, you know, talk to himself?"

The man looked at me questioningly, finished off his coffee before answering. "I couldn't tell. I was hunkered down in my vehicle until the police got there, as I imagine everyone else was. When I popped back up, the police were there dragging him out of the car with their guns drawn."

"That's a pretty serious case of road rage."

"The thing that still bugs me most about the whole situation is how calm he was when he got out to murder the guy. I got a fairly good look at his face as he walked up behind the Chevy."

He stopped talking and looked into my eyes. For the first time during his whole story, I saw genuine fear in his face.

"He had no expression whatsoever. It was like he had checked out emotionally. Those eyes of his held no recognition of any kind. I mean, don't get me wrong, I've seen pictures of Gacy and Dahmer, but their mugs are nothing compared to the devil's face I saw that day."

He stood up and put his ball cap back on, then began to walk out.

"Are you one-hundred percent sure he was talking to himself before he killed the guy?"

"I know what I saw."

"Thank you," I said. "You've helped out a lot. My name's Josh by the way."

He turned around and glanced back at me. "Jeremy."

"It was nice talking you, Jeremy."

"Same to you, son."

He made his exit and left me to my thoughts. Needless to say, any doubts I had about seeing the shadow or hearing it manipulate its victims flew out the window. I suddenly pictured myself in Jeremy's shoes. I was sitting in his semi and watching the guy in the Pontiac. His lips were moving, and I knew that sitting next to him, its form leaning over as if to whisper into his ear, was a shadow. It was telling him what to do and giving him several reasons to take out his revolver and silence the guy's horn-honking days forever.

I quickly finished my chips and tossed the bag into the receptacle at the front of the room. Then I proceeded to head back to my truck, deciding that I wanted to be back home.

The whole time I performed my check list before starting up the truck, I kept seeing the gunman's face in the café with the scar traveling down his cheek. His expression remained cold, without any hint of emotion. Suddenly, he turned his head, and the shadow hovering directly behind him became visible; it was ugly in its dark and hazy form, a head and shoulders with no defining features.

"*Shoot him,*" it said, "*Shoot him before he can stop you.*"

Then the man pointed the gun at my face and didn't smile or flinch when he pulled the trigger.

I shook my head, a damp chill spreading throughout my back. Beads of sweat rolled down my forehead, and I wiped them away, but the face remained; the face that did not smile, laugh or cry. The shadow hovered behind him, gloating.

By the time I started the truck and headed back toward familiar surroundings, I feared looking into my rearview mirror, terrified of finding a dark, vaporous form staring back without a face.

Chapter Seven

The next few days went by much faster than they should have. I felt like some kind of robot; the work I did was a mere act. I was on auto-pilot, but I still managed to receive and deliver several loads successfully, so much so that when Jimmy Barns, the owner of the company, came in for a surprise visit on a humid Thursday afternoon, I was one of the many drivers he talked to directly.

"You're an example of the kind of employee we need," he said, the smile he flashed revealing the amount of money he'd spent on a dentist.

Jimmy was a thin, charismatic older gentleman with a knack for flannel shirts and coveralls. He wasn't the ideal type one would think to own a professional company; yet despite his appearance, he was really smart. If there was an issue with one of the trucks, or the schedule seemed to be hampering the number of deliveries, he didn't hire someone to fix it. He simply took over and fixed it himself. He was probably rolling in cash, but you would never think it just by looking at him and listening to how humble he was.

So, here he was complimenting me for doing well when I wasn't even trying. Don't get me wrong; I love it when people let you know you're a good worker, but only if you truly deserve it. In all honesty, his praise made me feel really guilty. I think he picked up on my thoughts, too, because after the meeting was over, he pulled me aside.

"Was it something I said?" His face held concern.

"No."

"Is there some problem you're having?" He stepped closer, and whispered, "Maybe one of the other drivers? I know this isn't high school or anything, but people talk all the time. So if you've been of-fended in any way, even if it's one of the managers, please let me know."

"Thanks, but it's nothing. Really." I didn't know who I was trying to convince more, him or myself.

He nodded, but his face told me he didn't believe me totally. "If you ever need to talk, give me a call."

He handed me a business card with his cell phone number, and I accepted it, then politely excused myself, knowing that I would never at-tempt to use it.

Chapter Eight

What's interesting about the human psyche is how it deals with the inexplicable. As an avid reader, some of my favorite books deal with ghosts and the world's mysteries like Stonehenge and the construction of the Egyptian pyramids. The most popular genre for me, however, was the unsolved mysteries.

Growing up, I used to watch the TV show all the time, and I have fond memories of seeing real-life stories about haunted houses and people claiming to see angels, as well as impossible feats of strength that scientists could never explain.

The idea that there was a part of life that had no logical explanation intrigued me.

Now, I had the shadow-thing to try to make sense of. I kept coming back to the story I heard from Jeremy; there was no way he could have known about the incident from the café, and yet his experience almost matched mine to a tee, everything except his actually being able to see the shadow talking to the driver of the Pontiac.

I kept putting up road block after road block of logical explanations to try and understand what made no sense to me. Needless to say that after another two days of autopilot driving, I decided to use my off-days to do my own bit of research.

I visited the library at the University of Arkansas in Little Rock. It was the first time I ever visited that part of the city, and I decided afterward it would be my last. You'd think colleges would encourage visitors, but the parking was truly atrocious, so much so that it took me almost forty-five minutes to find a spot that ended up being almost a half-mile away.

The day was also muggy, even though the forecast called for rain later on. The clouds seemed to echo that prediction, and as I got out of my '91 Ford Tempo with so much paint peeling off it was most certainly a warrant wagon, they grew dense enough to blot out the sun.

It was still humid, though, and by the time I reached the library, my shirt was stuck to my body. A few female students wearing fairly revealing clothing exited the three sets of double-doors in front. As they walked by in their short-shorts, I began to wonder if they actually dressed like that to have guys rape them with their eyes.

The library was a triple-storied structure that reminded me of a small skyscraper due to the number of windows on each level. As I walked inside, wiping my forehead for the hundredth time, I looked past the metal detectors barring the entrance and beheld a large desk that took up more than thirty percent of the area on the first floor.

Six people were manning it: two younger men and four women. The men were busy stacking books on a pair of metal shelves directly behind the counter while the women kept watch. One of them, a red-haired beauty with modest attire—unlike the girls walking around the campus— was talking to a young man with a big, single-strap bag hanging at his right side. He was brandishing a thick book that I couldn't see the title of, but it seemed he was asking questions about it.

As I stepped closer, I caught the last bit of the conversation.

"I guess so," the red-haired librarian said, her eyes keeping focus on the person in front of her. "This book seems to cover a lot about biological theories surrounding cell tissue."

"Yes, but do you think I could take one of those theories and write about it for ten pages?"

"That depends on what you choose to focus on. Just check it out and give it a try."

He looked irritated that his question wasn't answered, but he quickly handed the book over and waited for her to scan it before handing it back to him.

"That's due back on the twenty-third, got it? Unless you renew it first."

The student nodded, accepted the book from her hand, and walked away. She then turned to me, and her eyes did a double-take, no doubt focusing on the dampness of my shirt and the sweat rolling down my face.

"I'm sure I look like death warmed over."

She smiled slightly. "You could say that. Let me guess, bad parking spot?"

"You should be a detective."

"It shows on your face," she said, pushing up a red pair of rimless glasses.

"Well, the visitor's parking is truly terrible here."

"Tell me about it; my friend George sometimes comes up here to use the computers, and he says he has to walk almost a mile from the parking lot."

"I believe him."

Her smile widened, and for a moment I considered what life would be like dating a college librarian. The thought quickly faded away at the sudden memory of Tracy's face. That smile and those warm lips, lips I would never kiss again.

I decided to quit wasting time and begin my search. "Hey, listen, do you have any books on famous serial killers or just downright evil people?"

My theory was simple. This shadow, or whatever it was, typically appeared when someone was in the midst of doing or (like with the cook at the diner) thinking about doing an evil action. I thought at first it must have been some kind of ghost or spirit, but that just seemed too simple. For one thing, this shadow didn't just stick to a single person like most hauntings are supposed to; no, it liked to jump to others like some kind of parasite, so I decided the best way to find evidence of it was to see if it had latched itself on to some famous individuals.

The cute librarian eyed me suspiciously but then grabbed one of the many pamphlets from a stand a few inches away from the counter. She leaned over, and I caught a faint whiff of some exotic perfume she wore; it reminded me of some fruit mixed with a dash of ocean water.

"Most of the true-crime volumes are up on the second floor," she said, taking up the pencil next to her to draw a crude circle on the second-floor section of the pamphlet. "Just take the elevator up and turn to your right once you exit. You should see the shelf about fifteen feet down that long hallway."

"Thanks." I grabbed the map from her. "I promise I'll put everything back when I'm finished."

She smiled, her lips slightly parted to expose a hint of pearl-white teeth. Obviously, she either had a really good dentist, or she was overly protective of them. This fascinated me, but I quickly turned away and walked to the elevator.

Her directions were spot on, and after stepping off and turning right, I found myself in a hallway lined with a seemingly never-ending series of bookshelves. One would need a ladder to reach some of the volumes, but I walked down through them, my eyes silently searching all the spines for hints of the word "crime."

I found what I sought a few moments later, and then I looked for an unoccupied table with a few chairs. Luckily there was one where the next series of shelves ended that created a nice intersection.

Venturing back to the shelf I saw earlier, I pulled the thickest book I saw. *50 Years of the Best True Crime* by Leonard Casey. I flipped it open and saw a smiling picture of an older gentleman in a suit and tie. His thick glasses reminded me of someone from the fifties. The author of the book appeared genuinely enthusiastic to bring such horrific stories to his readers.

I quickly skimmed through the pages, checking for any photos of the crime scenes or the killers themselves. I hit pay dirt about a quarter of the way in. The picture was of a slightly older man, thin as a rail and wearing one of those weird hats like one sees in England. Think Sherlock Holmes without the back flap and that's close enough. He was clean-shaven and smiling at the camera. He wore a pair of jean coveralls and an old jacket. "Ed Gein" the writer had written just below the photo. The name sounded familiar, but I couldn't remember why. I looked really hard at the picture but didn't see any misty form hovering behind him. Curiosity seizing me, however, I read over his history.

According to the author, this smiling gentleman liked to skin his victims and dry them out like hard leather, then he would wear them like Halloween masks or full body suits. I paused in my thoughts and tried to imagine being in his shoes. I pictured Gein standing there while one of his neighbors snapped a photo of him, his kind eyes hiding a deep need for horrifying acts.

I flipped back to the photo…

And dropped the book on the table loud enough to draw a few stares from another table of students nearby.

It was impossible.

There was Mr. Gein, his grin seemingly innocent and wholesome. His weird-looking hat slightly eschewed to the right side. He had his hand up in a friendly wave, but hovering behind him, slightly hidden by his body, was a dark, misty figure.

I brought a hand to my mouth, the image in front of me threatening to send me into a raving fit. The shadow hadn't been there before, I was sure of it; but there it was now, its faceless form mocking me.

A chill spread through my body like plague through Europe, and for the first time in almost seventeen years, I felt the front of my jeans grow warm with urine. The sensation of peeing myself was enough to con-vince me that the image in front of me was genuine. The spot wasn't too large on the front of my jeans, but it was definitely noticeable.

I kept glancing at the picture, expecting the shadow to disappear, but it remained. I wondered what it had said to Gein to convince him that he wanted to wear human skin like clothes, that killing the innocent people in this way was an act of charity.

Without thinking much, I began flipping pages, stopping every time another image appeared. "Jeffrey Dahmer" appeared in a single mug shot that was undoubtedly taken on his way into the prison system. I had heard the name before, like Gein's, but I couldn't remember what he'd done; I didn't stop to read his history—didn't need to. Behind his bored-looking expression in the orange jumpsuit he would wear 'til the day he died hov-ered a misty, dark figure. Again, there were no eyes or a mouth, yet I knew that when that photo was being snapped, that shadow was whispering into Dahmer's ears.

I shuddered to think about what it was telling him.

More pictures found me. Names I somewhat knew but never learned about, such as Ted Bundy, Charles Manson, and Theodore White. The shadow behind Bundy was barely visible, but the two—that's right, you heard me correctly—behind Manson's stern face full of long hair and bush-like beard seemed to be cheering him on, telling him all the good he was doing with his unholy sacrifices and brutal murders.

I stopped on Theodore White's picture. There was something much different here than any of the previous ones. In the shot, a police officer had just handcuffed Mr. White after discovering an old lady he had sexually assaulted and beaten to death with a brick. His face was turned toward the reporter's camera, yet his eyes were unmoving and lifeless.

On the surface, the picture seemed fairly normal, but what made me stop in the first place, and what now sent a fresh shiver up my spine, was what the shadow was doing. Or at least what it appeared to be doing. It hovered over to the side, almost out of frame, but a large, funnel-like appendage had sprouted out of it and attached itself to White's face.

What was it giving White?

Or what was it taking away from him?

This new behavior was more disturbing than the basic appearances I had observed in the shadow from the diner and the ones featured on the other killers in the book. Another thought suddenly occurred to me. If I could see the misty figures in the books, didn't it stand to reason that others could, too?

I decided to use my cell phone to capture the various faces in the book. After getting what I needed, I skimmed through them to make sure the shadows were still visible; they were. Satisfied, I put the book back and proceeded down the hallway towards the elevator.

A young man dressed in a Grateful Dead t-shirt and blue jeans was just getting off. I started to walk past him but stopped. There was some-thing about him that felt wrong. He passed me and kept walking, so I turned to get another look. It was then that I saw the dark, misty figure clinging to his back.

I started toward him, trying to get close enough to hear if the thing was talking to him, when a young woman came around the corner and bumped into me, sending both of us falling backward. I didn't bother to apologize when I saw she was already getting to her feet, a look of annoyance on her face. Instead, I looked back at my target, then blinked a few times to make sure I wasn't imagining what I saw.

The shadow was gone, and the awkward feeling along with it.

It was time to leave the library. After taking the elevator back down and stepping off, I didn't attempt to acknowledge the wave the cute red-headed librarian gave me and simply half-walked, half-sprinted through the set of doors and back out into the grueling heat of the afternoon.

Chapter Nine

I decided to tell Fred about the shadows. I hadn't been spending much time with him lately, partly due to our differing driving schedules and the fact that I was now in my own place, a small one-bedroom nightmare that I was sure would be lost as soon as building inspectors came to look at the surrounding area.

That didn't stop me from inviting him over one afternoon once he drove back in. I had picked up a couple of twelve packs of Bud Lite, just in case he decided I was insane; I could then blame it on the beer. Turns out I didn't have to, and by the time I finished showing him the photos and told him about the café experience, he seemed genuinely surprised, but not the kind of surprise that denoted a lack of belief.

He held my phone and looked closely at the photo of Theodore White.

"Well," I said, "do you see it?"

"Not really."

"What do you mean 'not really'?" I took another quick swig of beer and slammed it back down on the wooden table, sending splatters of it all through the air. "You either see it, or you don't."

"There's nothing there but White's face."

"Give it back to me." I snatched it and took a look myself. The strange figure with the funnel appendage was still there. "You're blind!" I thrust the phone back at him. "It's there as plain as day!"

He shook his head. "I'm sorry, man. I just don't see it."

I could feel the warmth on my face from the beer getting stronger, and along with it, my own frustration. The shadow was there for everyone to see, but why was I the only one given the privilege (or the curse)? Nothing made sense anymore.

Fred tried to pass off my ravings to an overworked and exhausted mind. "Look, man, you've been working yourself to death since I brought you into this company. Maybe you need a break?"

"I'm telling you I'm perfectly fine."

"I don't know," he said, and pushed his glasses up. "You're beginning to sound a lot like Charles."

"What?"

"Yeah. The other drivers like to gossip in the break rooms a lot, you know." He smiled, and I suddenly felt uncomfortable. "Well, when Charles was training me, we stopped to grab a few bags of chips from the vending machines, and an overweight driver was sitting at one of the tables next to it. He wore a thick leather jacket and had an unlit cigarette dangling from the left corner of his mouth. Kinda rough looking if you catch my drift."

"I do," I said, my unease steadily growing. "Keep going."

He coughed and took a swig from his open beer, swallowed, and put it back on the table. "Well, like I was saying, this guy spied us as we came in to grab some chips, and he leaned toward me as I was putting money in the machine. 'Old Charles told you about his shadow buddies yet?' he said, and I pushed the combination I wanted before I asked him what he was talking about. 'Let Charles tell you,' he said, and turned to him. 'Well, how about it?' By this time, Charles had his bag and stepped up to join me. I didn't really care for the look on his face. As you've seen, Charles is usually always smiling, especially while he's training."

"Yeah, he does at that," I said.

"Well, he wasn't smiling then, and I thought he and this rough-looking guy were going to come to blows. The other guy didn't seem to notice or care because he kept right on talking. 'Tell him, Charles. There's shadows stalking us right now, right?' Charles looked at me and said 'Let's go,' but before we could, the guy stood up with a big grin on his face. 'Don't you know, rookie, ol' Charles here can see shadow ghosts or demons or whatever he calls them. Ain't that right?' I looked over at Charles, and I swear the man was livid. He kept giving me the 'Let's go' expression.

"Well, I finally listened and grabbed my Doritos. The overweight man just kept cackling like a hyena or something, but Charles never responded. Instead, he walked back out, and I followed him."

"Did he say anything to you about the shadows or ghosts?" I was squeezing my can hard enough that it was sending pain through my hand. "I have to know!"

"No, man." Fred took one last swig of his beer and then tossed the can into the receptacle near the wall. "He never mentioned anything about it. But when I asked a few other drivers the next time I was in the break room, they told me that Charles had overworked himself at one point and began hallucinating. They told me he'd see shadows hanging off people and claimed these figures would talk to him."

I let go of my beer and scanned the photos in my phone. The shadows were still there, almost daring me to keep pursuing them.

"I'm concerned about you, man."

"I'm not crazy," I said, and looked up, focusing my attention on him. "And I don't think he was either."

Chapter Ten

It took almost a week before I saw Charles in his office. He was in the middle of training a few newcomers. I got to see one of them; an older woman with rounded hips and long, salt-and-pepper hair kept in a ponytail. She exited his office as I walked up the set of stairs, gave me a quick glance, and then kept right on moving, down the stairs and out of sight.

Charles stood in the open doorway, a sly grin posted on his slightly weathered face. He wore a pair of suspenders that reminded me of Ed Gein's in that photo, and it was enough to make me feel uncomfortable.

"I think I may have to give her some more attention. What do you think?"

The thought of those two going at it almost brought my lunch back up, but I simply smiled back. "Hey, all's fair in love and war."

"Ain't that the truth," he said, then turned back around and took a few steps into his office. "So, what can I do for you today?"

"Do you mind if I close the door?" He stopped before reaching his seat, turned back, and gave me a concerned look. I persisted, however. "I really want to keep this just between us."

He turned back and walked over to a large computer chair with thick armrests, sat down, leaned back, and placed his hands behind his head. "I suppose so. Seems you've got something weighing heavy on you."

"Thanks," I said, pushing the door until it latched. I quickly drew the blinds and found a seat in front of his large wooden desk. He watched me as I sat down, his eyes never relinquishing their concern.

"So," he said, as I finally took my seat and faced him. "What's the problem?"

I had thought long and hard the previous few days about how to begin before requesting the meeting, but nothing really seemed right. So, I decided to try a direct approach.

"When did you start seeing them?"

His expression changed slightly, and the level of concern seemed more prominent, especially in his eyes. "Them? Who are you talking about?"

I leaned closer and rested my forearms on the desk. "You know who I mean. The shadows."

The concern evaporated and what replaced it was a combination of fear and anger. This was going to be a tough conversation to have, but I was willing to pry as much as I needed to.

"Who told you about that?" Charles sat upright and placed both hands on the desk. He was a slightly intimidating figure like this, especially when he wasn't smiling anymore.

"It doesn't matter. I'm not here to make fun of you or call you crazy."

His face softened, but the wrinkles around his eyes dug deeper.

"You've seen them, too, haven't you," he said.

I nodded and brought out my cell phone. The pictures were saved in a new folder so they were easier to find. Once opened, I handed it to him. He studied the pictures for a few moments then glanced back up at me.

"You can see them in the pictures, right?"

"Yes," he said, his eyes wide with alarm. "They're there."

"I need to know what I'm seeing. Nothing makes any sense to me."

"I felt the same way at first," he said, and handed the phone back to me. "I still do."

"Do you know what they are?"

"First off, tell me about when you first encountered one."

I told him about the small diner and the shooter with the emotionless face and eyes. The shadow that kept telling him what he needed to do and why. Charles didn't look that surprised, and by the time I mentioned what the old man at the other depot told me about the crazy driver in the Pontiac, I had a feeling he had seen this all before.

After I finished, Charles sank back in the chair. "Thank God you came to me."

"Why?"

"I was beginning to think I was going crazy after all."

"Who knows, maybe we're both experiencing the same kind of illness." I shrugged my shoulders.

"No, I doubt that. I actually went to see a doctor and had a C.A.T. scan done, but it found nothing."

"So, you're telling me these shadows, or spirits, or whatever, are the real deal?"

"I'm not sure these things are simply shadows or spirits now," he said. He slowly got to his feet and walked around the corner of the desk. "What you described happened with the chef at the diner kind of changes everything."

"How so?"

"Think about what happened at the diner with the cook." He stepped to the side of my chair, his arms crossed behind his back. He seemed to have gained a little weight since I'd last seen him. "What does that suggest about the shadow or entity or whatever it is?"

"That it can change its focus very quickly."

"Right! That's not something I've ever heard of a ghost doing before. Typically, all the hauntings I've ever read about or watched in movies are centered on a location and a particular person, not some random diner or the middle of a traffic jam."

"So, what are they then?"

Charles shook his head. "I don't know."

"This is useless."

I started to get up, but he placed a hand on my shoulder and held me down. "No, it's not. Your pictures prove you and I aren't crazy."

"That's just great," I said, sitting back down so he didn't have to keep his hand on my shoulder. "So we both know these things are really out there. Bravo! But that doesn't explain them."

"Maybe it does, though. Maybe there's some kind of connection we can't see yet."

"So, what do we do?"

"I'll tell you what I did."

I listened with every fiber of my being, hoping the man in front of me had found some kind of talismanic power to ward off all evil.

"I let it go," he said, and then walked over to the door and grabbed the knob. "As I think you should."

Anger boiled inside me, threatening to explode all over him. "How can you say that? There's a world only you and I can see, and even after all the weird, messed-up things occurring because of it, all you can say is forget about it?"

"That's right." He turned back to me, and his face looked much older than he actually was. The lines dug deeper into his face, almost making them appear to be superficial gashes in the skin. His eyes narrowed to slits, and the anger I felt gave way to unease, then to out-right fear. "I have a feeling you and I have been gifted, or cursed, if you will. We're seeing something that has always existed, something that was supposed to remain hidden from human eyes and understanding."

"But why? Don't you want to know? What if these shadows are secretly causing every evil action? I mean…what if one of these things is what told some punk to shoot at the apartments where Tracy and I were staying!"

Charles lowered his head. "I heard about that. I am so sorry for your loss, but finding out its cause won't solve anything, will it?"

"Maybe not, but knowing why it occurred would help me sleep better at night. Besides, who knows, I might be able to catch one of these things and torture it for a while."

Charles opened the door and motioned for me to leave. I got up and walked toward him, my eyes boring into his. He frowned, and as I stepped out into the hallway, he said something that gave me pause, if only for the briefest of moments. "Right now you and I are like children in our rooms, watching a horror movie through a tiny crack in the door. Ask yourself this: if the little bits and pieces we've already seen are enough to cause us several sleepless nights, do you really want to push that door all the way open?"

I didn't have a response.

Anger soon replaced the fear, and I walked quickly down the stairs toward the front of the building. My mind raced, each individual thought a new reality of possibility. I was so involved in my own thought processes, I barely took any notice of Fred as he passed me. I heard him talking, but his words were simply white noise on a big TV screen with no picture. I simply said, "Okay, see you later," and kept walking.

By the time I walked through the front door and back out into the sunlight, I had already made up my mind.

I was going to open my bedroom door once and for all.

I just needed to figure out how.

Chapter Eleven

My '91 Ford Tempo was bad about dying when I let it idle. This was a huge problem because my apartment sat near the main road, and I had to pass under several lights to reach it.

As I feared it might, it died on me two lights away from my street. Luckily, the street was devoid of traffic, which was strange. The sound of drums and cheering caught my attention suddenly. Judging by its intensity, the activity was not far in the distance. A parade of some sort. That explained the lack of traffic.

I turned the key, and the car whined for a few moments but didn't do anything. Anger swelled inside, and I pictured a full can of gasoline and a lit match, then a blazing car and my own laughter. I tried the key again, and after a few whines, the engine turned over and began to hum and cough. This vehicle was living on borrowed time, but I silently prayed it would last at least a few more months.

As I drove through the last two lights, I saw the detour signs blocking the next intersection. There were lots of people standing on both sides, while the street had become a runway for colorful floats decorated with various colors. I could only make out two large ones, and both of them were blue all over with giant beach balls sitting on their sides. The one closest to me had a volleyball net in the center while its relative had a crudely constructed sandcastle that didn't look like it was made of sand. Several children sat on the floats, all dressed alike, in blue shirts and yellow shorts.

I admired that they still put on the summer parade with the heat being as intense as it was, and I smiled as I let off the brake and turned down the street leading to my apartment.

When I walked in the door, I began to think about how I was going to find one of the shadow things. At first, I thought about walking up to the parade and just scanning the crowds. Surely one person would have one hovering near them—like the student with the Grateful Dead t-shirt had.

I opened the fridge and pulled the last can of Bud Lite from the bottom shelf, popped it open, took a quick swig, and sat down at the table.

I thought about the people at the parade, then the gunman at the diner, and a chill crept up my back. I imagined the man with that cold, emotionless face standing in front of the procession as it crept by, a shadow hovering behind him. Then it leaned over to whisper in his ear, but he was too far away for me to hear. There was a flash of brightness as he brought out a long assault rifle and aimed it at all those smiling faces. Then the steady drone of automatic gunfire as he sprayed in a semi-circle. I started to run toward him, but someone in the crowd drew my attention away: a thin woman standing a few feet to his right. Her belly was swollen with child, and she caressed it with her right hand.

"No," I shouted, the steady stream of bullets all but drowning out my words. "Tracy! Get away!"

Then the man with the emotionless face turned in her direction.

I shut my eyes and waited for the tell-tale sounds of death.

My mind took me away from the parade then and back to my old apartment. I pictured Tracy sitting there in the living room, patting her stomach as she read a lively novel. I saw her eyes scanning the pages, a speed-reader's style. Then a sudden loud report, and she feels a few stings—not overly painful—and can no longer hold the book.

She stops patting her belly and wonders why she feels so warm all the sudden, and why the warmth is sliding down her clothes. Then she finds herself looking up at the ceiling for some reason, unable to move…

And then, nothing.

Tears welled up, and I wiped them away hard enough to cause irritation. I had to know, then. Even after all I had seen and heard and felt, I wasn't going to stop until I knew. Going to the parade was too risky, but there had to be another way. Charles's face appeared in my mind, and his words filled my senses. "Maybe there's some kind of connection we can't see yet."

I kept repeating these words, my mind scanning every syllable for any connection I might have missed. I pulled my phone out and opened the folder containing the pictures from the book. Several faces flashed by, all in various states of expression. The only thing that never changed was the shadows hovering behind and to the sides of them. I came to Theodore White's picture. Him in cuffs and staring icily at the camera, the shadow reaching a funnel-like appendage towards him, as if to drink from—

His crimes!

My eyes widened.

"That's it!" I shouted, and my voice echoed off the walls. "That's the connection!"

I quickly flipped to the other pictures: Ed Gein's photo had been taken by a neighbor before his final murder that ended up with his capture. Charles Manson's picture was taken at the prison, after the acts that landed him there. Bundy and Dahmer's were the same way. All prison shots, after the crimes.

All except Theodore White. His photo was taken at the scene of the murder. In fact, I learned that he was just walking out when the police cruiser that took him into custody pulled up. He had just finished his heinous act on the elderly woman.

I zoomed in on the photo. There were bloodstains on White's street clothes. Red and unquestionably fresh. The shadow was hovering to the side, a large, dark funnel attached to White's emotionless face.

"It's feeding off of him," I said to myself, and was both excited yet unnerved. The final piece of the puzzle had fallen into my hands. I thought about the diner; the gunman had shot the poor man with the umbrella, yet the shadow didn't feed. Instead, it leapt from him to the chef, then tried to get him to commit murder. It only went away when—

"I stopped it."

That's it, it wasn't finished! It wanted the chef more than the gunman, for some reason, or—

"Maybe it felt it could get two for the price of one?"

It didn't matter anymore. I had what I needed. The thing's purpose, so far as I could tell, was to manipulate its victims into committing evil actions, such as the gunman in the café and even the road rager in the Pontiac.

There was just one thing that still baffled me: How did it pick someone to feed off of?

Then it finally came to me, and even if the world had decided to end at that very moment, it wouldn't have been enough to wipe away the grin on my face.

Chapter Twelve

I stood in front of the bathroom mirror, the same pistol Tracy's father had given her, the one she never got a chance to use, clutched in my right hand. The weight of it gave me comfort, and I pictured Tracy sitting in the chair, her lifeless eyes glaring up at the ceiling; her soul—as well as our unborn son's—leaving her body and not knowing why.

Anger built quickly, then rage. I saw myself pointing the gun at someone, an unknown without a face. I saw the black car, its driver faceless like the one hanging out of the window holding an assault rifle.

"I want to kill them," I said to the mirror. I closed my eyes, allowed the rage to guide me. "I want to fire this pistol into their faces until there are no more bullets left. Then I'll reload it and fire into them again."

A coldness spread through my body all of a sudden. My anger began to evaporate, along with every other feeling I had. I couldn't be mad anymore, couldn't cry, or laugh. I just waited, my eyes shut to my own existence.

"*Yes*," said a cold, hollow voice behind me. "*You will… for Tracy. And for Timothy.*"

"Timothy?" I kept my eyes closed.

"*That's what she was planning to name him.*"

I opened my eyes, and although every muscle on my face seemed frozen and gave me a lifeless expression, fear found me again. There, hovering behind me in the mirror, its misty form solid enough to send new chills through my body, was a shadow. Its humanoid shape seemingly mimicked my own, as if we were brothers. In a way, now that I look back on it, I guess we were. There was no insecurity or possible trick of the light. The being behind me was as real as the gun I held, only much colder than the handle of the pistol.

I regained my composure after a few moments, locked my eyes on the space that seemed to be the thing's head.

"What are you?" I asked. "I have to know."

The shadowy form drifted to the left of me, its coldness threatening to consume my whole being. It settled itself once more, and a small appendage fell across my shoulder.

"*I'm what you want,*" the thing said. "*What you* really *are.*"

"Are you the source of all evil?"

The thing cackled, its poisonous voice seemingly filling the whole apartment. "*That's a question for the Man Upstairs,*" it said, mimicking my father's voice.

I turned to face it. The interior of the bathroom was now a pulsing black mist that enveloped most of the space next to the bathtub. The shadow's length stretched all the way to the floor and split in the middle, creating the impression of separate legs.

I lifted the pistol and pointed it at the misty form. "You took away everything important in my life."

"*I only encourage, I do not force.*"

The pistol shook in my hands. I tightened my finger around the trigger, my mind racing. I wanted to hear the gun go off, to tear a gaping hole in this thing that was mocking my life's miseries, to shut it up once and for all.

The thing cackled again, louder this time.

"So you make things worse!" My anger returned, all of it focused on the misty form in front of me.

"*Only to make sure there is plenty to feed on.*"

Again I debated pulling the trigger. If this thing was telling the truth, its purpose was an abomination upon all humanity.

"I should end you right now."

The shadow drifted closer, bringing an almost crippling coldness with it. "*They're close by,*" it said. "*I can take you to them.*"

The pressure I had been putting on the trigger subsided, and my anger resurfaced, this time pointed in a different direction. "Where are they? Tell me!"

"*Follow me,*" the misty form uttered, and then it abruptly drifted past me and out into the hallway. The chill left the bathroom, and I found it much easier to move, so I followed it.

I watched from the hallway as it drifted into the living room, past the empty beer can on the table, and directly through the front door. A chill crawled through my spine like an army of spiders, each touch of their hairy legs sending waves of coldness up my vertebrae. Still, I followed it, out the door and into the heat of the afternoon. It hovered past my car and started down the sidewalk, out towards the street. I knew where it was going, but I didn't ask any questions. I just kept picturing Tracy's face, her lifeless eyes, and that familiar coldness welled up within me, shutting down every emotion I had.

I tucked the pistol into my pocket and continued to follow the figure as it passed through the detour sign and continued up the street. The sounds of loud music and drums filled the air, along with children laughing.

"*Almost there,*" the thing said, and I thought I sensed elation in its voice.

The parade was going full swing. A large float that was made up to look like a sandcastle rolled slowly down the road while a large group of kids dressed in Karate uniforms, the two in the front row holding American flags, followed behind it.

I walked through the large crowd that had gathered on the street and kept moving, pushing several children and older women out of my way. The shadow moved faster, and I couldn't keep up with it anymore. A deep, sinking feeling filled my heart, but my expression never changed.

Suddenly, I pushed through the people in front of me and caught sight of the misty figure again. It was standing on the other side of the street, directly behind two teenagers. They were both wearing tank tops and jean shorts. The one on the left, however, had a dark blue bandanna tied around his head.

I froze in my tracks and pictured them riding down the street in a black car. I then saw the one without the bandanna hanging out the window holding an assault rifle. He aimed it at the few houses and apartments, his emotionless face hiding the joy he felt as he pulled the trigger.

"*Yes*," the shadow cried out to me. "*This is them.*"

The next few moments were over very quickly, but they seemed to happen in slow motion. I started walking across the street, and when I was about six feet from them—the one with the bandanna's face suddenly showed some alarm while the other one was too busy trying to chat with an attractive blonde beside him—I pulled the pistol from my pocket, aimed, and started firing.

The first shot went wild and broke off a piece of bark in the old oak tree behind the road. The next one hit home, and a red dot quickly blossomed into a red rose on the bandanna-less teenager's tank top. He turned toward me, a look of disbelief on his face, but then started to reach into his pants pocket.

I fired again, and the middle of his face caved in, sending blood and bone all over the woman he'd been talking to. By this time, people began to scream and grab their children. Many of them ducked down and lay flat on the ground as I shifted my attention to the one in the bandanna.

"*Watch out*," the shadow said.

The other teenager had a snub-nosed revolver in his hand, and as I fired the first of several rounds at him, he let loose on me. The first shot whizzed by my right temple and found its mark in a young mother trying to flee with her daughter. His second shot caught me in the left shoulder.

The pain was exquisite, but I managed to get two more rounds off in quick succession, one which hit him in the stomach, causing his next shot to graze my side, before the next one went through his left eye and blew a hole—similar in size to one police later found on the poor mother that had been hit while trying to flee—through the back of his head.

I continued to fire, riddling his still-standing body with holes. It was only when the gun clicked empty that I stopped, and by that time most of the crowds were far enough away that their screams weren't loud enough to hurt my now-ringing ears. The two teenagers lay dead on the edge of the sidewalk; the first one had a small pistol similar to my own clutched in his hand that he'd never gotten a chance to fire, while the other one's barrel was still smoking. His blue bandanna was barely clinging to his forehead, and as I fell to my knees, the pain from my wounds over-whelming me, the wind tore it loose and sent it drifting down the street.

The dark, misty figure was still hovering in the same spot, but it suddenly drifted slowly towards me. "*Well done.*"

Then I saw something, something that still haunts me.

Before a couple of police officers arrived, the shadow began to change. Not just change, but rather *materialize*. The misty figure became solid, and the darkness of its body took on fleshy overtones.

Its skin glistened as if it was made of plastic, and what appeared to be veins protruded all over its body. The head appeared human, but it was devoid of hair, and it held no eyes or nose, just a mouth that stretched al-most the entire circumference of its face.

The body itself was humanoid, with two arms and two distinct legs, but that's where the similarities ended. There were thick claws on the ends of its fingers, and its feet reminded me of those of the velociraptors I'd seen in *Jurassic Park*, only there were five toes, each ending in scythe-like claws.

The pain in my shoulder was spreading, and I wanted so badly to collapse, but I forced myself to stay alert. The fleshy being turned its face with the massive mouth toward me.

"What are you," I asked, every word producing more pain than I'd ever experienced before.

That unnaturally long mouth devoid of any lips spread open like a freshly made gash as it spoke: "*I'm hungry.*"

The thing's chest split open, the skin peeling apart to reveal a pink, slime-covered funnel covered in needle-like teeth. The appendage that forced its way out into the sunlight was attached to some kind of intestine-like tube that disappeared within swirling mounds of flesh.

All I could do was watch, my eyes wide and my lips trembling, as that glistening, flesh-colored instrument of horror drifted toward my face.

Chapter Thirteen

"The last thing I remember before I woke up in this hospital, hand-cuffed to this bed, was the creature's laughter.

"It followed me into my dreams, and I can still hear it now, even in this room. I don't know why it chose to reveal its true self to me, officer, but it's like I can feel it now, deep down inside.

"I'll bet you think I'm crazy, right? Well, if that's true, why can I see that misty form hovering behind you right now? I know what it's telling you. That your wife is having an affair with your neighbor, that they have been staining your bed sheets for the past six months while you're at work. It's trying to convince you that a crime of passion is no crime at all, that no jury would convict you if you were to walk in on them after you leave here and plant a bullet in each of their foreheads.

"Don't listen to it, officer. Don't make the same mistake I did.

"Wait! Where are you going? No, stop listening to it!

"Come back! Come back!"

GRAVE MARKER

A.P. SESSLER

BRAIN ATTACK

Acknowledgments

Thanks to part-time and full-time Canucks Derik Foster and Jo-Anne Russell for helping me Canadianize this story, and apologies where I've taken liberties.

Chapter One

Jarred Galway sat strapped to the chair, his bloody wrists and bruised ankles rendered immobile by the men surrounding him. Between he and his captors sat a small table with a glass half-full of water, the damnedest time for a metaphor, but it gave him a snicker. The sole light bulb dangling from the ceiling just above him painted his antagonists as silver-lined shadows.

One of the shadows stepped closer, enough into the light for Jarred to see the leather-clad arms and bare hands retrieve from an interior pocket a pair of black leather gloves, which they preceded to don.

"The rest of you can leave," said the man in a gentle, disarming voice. "I'll handle this."

The shadows retreated into the dark, half a dozen shoes shuffling across the floor, then an unseen door creaked open and shut.

Sweat ran down Jarred's bare crown, stinging his eyes.

"Now, Mister Galway. I want you to know there is absolutely nothing to worry about. You'll be perfectly fine, *as long as* you cooperate."

"Sure," said Jarred, his voice deep and stony, like the inside of a long-empty well. "But if you don't mind, can I ask the first question?"

The shape stooped over, and a bald head with gleaming glasses leaned into the light. He smiled, his mustache curving in perfect parallel. "It's a little unorthodox, but go ahead."

Jarred stared at the glass. "Just one thing. Are all the pricks from Psi-Corp as ugly as you??" he said and glanced at him.

The man's smile disappeared, and then his face as he stood straight, back into the shadow. A glint of light shone on leather as the back of his gloved hand struck Jarred's cheek.

Jarred's head snapped back and his chest heaved with angered breaths. He leaned forward with a sinister smile, his lips bloodied. "Not bad. Now I got something for you." He dropped his head, almost as if bowing, but there was nothing courteous or humbled in his intent.

The sound of breath escaping the interrogator's lungs preceded arms falling to his side, fists clenched. He fought to open his hands, to reach for the gun strapped to his hip, but he was only able to paw at it like a clumsy animal.

A voice came over a loudspeaker. "Something wrong?"

The struggle for air continued, and soon the man stepped back into the light, his eyes and jaws closed tight. A high-pitched sound filled his ears and rose and rose and rose, ascending to a level high above the threshold of human hearing into an ultrasonic hell of endless and soundless agony.

His face turned beet-red, then purple. His convulsing arms struck the table, tipping the glass over and spilling its contents onto the floor, all while Jarred sat with the same sinister look, frozen in place like a statue caught in Medusa's glare.

"We're coming in," the voice said over the loudspeaker.

With just a glance, and still strapped to his chair three meters away, Jarred locked the door; the sound of tumblers falling into place echoed in the room.

"He's too powerful," said one of the men.

"Get the keys," said another.

"What do you think I'm doing?" the first snapped back.

Jarrod threw another glance toward the door.

"Ow!" the first man shouted.

"What is it?"

"It burned my hand."

"What do you mean?"

"Look at the doorknob! It's red hot!"

There was a grunt and a thud and the door bowed. Another grunt and the door sprung open, and men rushed in with guns drawn.

Like a skilled singer reaching for a high note, Jarred's mind ascended to the sweet, sweet frequency he had been searching for, his lips puckering in satisfied amusement.

The man in leather opened his eyes to see his restrained conqueror just before his head swelled to four times its size and exploded in a fiery, burning-hot orgasm of blood and brain, coating the dangling light bulb in crimson and turning everything and everyone in the room red.

The terrified men turned their guns upon their prisoner, who, with but a glance in their direction, forced them to turn their guns upon one another and empty the clips in a barrage of bullets. Monochromatic blood burst from their chests in slow-motion, then froze in still-frame as a font typical of '70s computer printouts appeared one green letter at a time, filling a third of the screen:

BRAIN ATTACK

A moment later, the action reversed. Blood entered holes in chests and flaps of skin closed up into perfectly sound jackets with a series of bright flashes. The men backed out through the doorway, and the whole room went from red to black, the light bulb from red to white, and the red, gray, white, and pulpy yellow contents of the nameless man's head flew from every direction back into his swollen head, and then froze again in an interlaced image of two blurred frames.

A finger pointed at the computer monitor where the frozen image sat. On the desk beside the computer sat a closed DVD case with an illustrated version of the very same image with the title BRAIN ATTACK superimposed over it.

"Him," said Ron, seated at his desk in the dimly lit office.

He wore his long, dark hair in a ponytail. Behind him, a framed Master's degree graced the wall, left of a bookcase lined not with best-sellers on business and marketing, but with collectible figurines from classic slasher films.

Looking over his shoulder was a slender fellow with short, dark red, curly locks. He laughed. "Head-Explode Guy?" said Franklin.

Ron nodded enthusiastically. "Exactly."

"Good luck. No one knows who he is."

"Just look up—"

"IMDB? Did it. And the movie credits on every home release to date. Nothing. There's a conspiracy theory that Owensby swept him under the rug because he died during filming."

"How?"

"Fayman blew his brains out. For real."

Ron spun around in his chair to face Franklin. "Shot him?"

"No, I mean brain attack. Hence, the film's namesake."

"Bull."

"Yeah, but it's a great story, eh?"

They laughed.

"Well, here's the deal, Frank. You're my go-to trivia man. I know you can find out who this guy is. Do your thing, bring me a name, and I'll do mine. I'll get him."

"I'll try, but don't hold your breath."

"Come on, Frank. I'm counting on you. We need Head-Explode Guy to make this Horr-Onto the best Horr-Onto ever. And *he's* gonna make it happen."

"Okay. I'll get on it."

"That's my boy."

"Now, if I'm going to spend a whole day scouring every possible source," Franklin raised a finger for emphasis, "including microfiche if necessary, I would really appreciate it if you get the website and fliers looking A-plus." His raised finger met his thumb in an okay sign. "Can you do that for me?"

Ron clicked on the movie player window and dragged it left of the computer's desktop, revealing a graphics app window with a work in progress. "I'm on it now. But you know..." he said as he stared at the fuzzy still image on his laptop screen with a dissatisfied frown. "...I thought the DVD would be clearer."

Franklin shrugged. "Should have bought the Blu-ray."

Chapter Two

The smell of coffee and cinnamon wafted through Timmy's, accompanied by the gurgling of cappuccino machines. Ron sat at a table in front of a bay window. He sipped a double-double English toffee and nibbled a honey cruller.

In the glare of his laptop, he saw his reflection. He wiped his chinless mouth with a napkin, releasing a lip full of crumbs to settle into the crease of the t-shirt covering his large gut. Remnants of the napkin, as well as some stubborn crumbs, clung to his unshaven face, forcing him to wipe his mouth a second time with his forearm.

He shook his head in frustration and looked past his reflection at the latest numbers on Horr-Onto.com's Admin page.

Hits:	2,486
Interested:	1,505
Tickets purchased:	731

He reached the bottom of the screen, where the angular outlines of several mountain ranges declared the aforementioned details in a horizontal timeline. They had grown taller on a weekly basis. He smiled.

"What are you grinning about?" the voice came from his left.

"Frank!" Ron greeted his partner. "We just broke 700 in ticket sales."

Franklin nodded. "Good news. But not as good as my news," he said, and took a seat opposite Ron.

"Well, it's been two days, so I hope it's good."

Franklin pulled the laptop bag from his shoulder and sat it on the table. "Just finish your donut while I break it down."

"It's a cruller," Ron clarified, crumbs falling from his full mouth.

With a sharp and deliberately annoyed motion, Franklin swept the crumbs from the table before pulling his laptop out of the bag and setting it down. "You're killing me. Just eat and watch. And keep the crumbs on your side of the table."

Ron shrugged.

Franklin cycled through a series of commercial clips on YouTube, all featuring a familiar bald man. "Eh?"

Ron smiled in amazement. "Is that Head-Explode Guy?"

Franklin sighed. "No, it's my Uncle Milton. Of *course,* it's Head-Explode Guy!"

"Okay, okay. You have a name?"

Franklin shook his head. "Why do you so doubt my skills? I told you I had good news, didn't I?"

Franklin clicked on the CADB.com tab of his web browser and pointed to the screen.

Ron mumbled as he read. "Commercial Actors Database? Okay." His eyes found the line Franklin pointed at. "Daniel Lewis ... Disgruntled Customer. Okay, but there's no picture."

"Well yeah, the commercial is thirty years old. Now look at this," Franklin said, and entered another product name. Using the touch-pad, he scrolled down and pointed again.

"Daniel Lewis ... Boss," Ron read. "Okay, still no picture. How do we know it's him?"

Franklin flipped back to the YouTube tab and typed Daniel Lewis in the search bar.

A series of thumbnails lined the search results, mostly the commercials they had already viewed. A clip in the middle of the page was titled "Is this the same Dan Lewis?" and featured the iconic image from Brain Attack.

"And I thought *we* had a lot of time on our hands," said Ron. "Who made this connection?"

"Some guy living in his mother's basement? I don't know. The point is, this is him. Dan Lewis *is* Head-Explode Guy."

Franklin closed his laptop, leaned back in his seat, and crossed his arms. "Eh?"

Ron smiled and nodded. "Good work. I knew you could do it. Now, how do we contact him?"

"Okay. Don't get mad, but here's where the trail runs cold."

"What? You got my hopes up just to—"

Franklin raised a finger. "Not finished. While exhausting every possible connection, I stumbled upon ... Are you ready for it?"

Ron rolled his eyes.

"Are you ready? You're sitting down so you must be ready," Franklin teased.

"Just say it already! Jesus Murphy," Ron grumbled, and reached for his English toffee.

"I just so happened to get John Fayman's address," he mumbled.

Ron choked on the sip. Before he finished coughing, he choked out the words "You what?"

"I got John Fayman's address. Who needs Dan Lewis when we got John Fayman?"

"We don't *have* John Fayman. We have his *address*."

"It's as good as in the bag. The guy hasn't done anything since *Brain Attack*. He literally dropped off the map."

"Figuratively."

"Figuratively dropped off the map," Franklin corrected himself. "Until now."

He removed a piece of paper from his jacket pocket, unfolded it, and held it up in both hands for Ron to see.

Ron squinted his eyes at the mesh of printed lines running to and fro. He soon perceived it was a literal map. "Jesus Murphy, it's way up in the mountains. You know I hate road trips."

Franklin handed him the map and smiled. "Save your gas receipts. They're a business expense."

Chapter Three

With one hand on the steering wheel, Ron glanced at the map as he neared a series of exits on the interstate. He returned the map to the passenger seat and his right hand to the wheel.

The traffic wasn't bad, with most of the cars speeding past and giving him a wide berth, except for the white van to his left. It kept pace with him, changing lanes in parallel. He felt like their vehicles were part of some unknown caravan.

He pulled right to take the exit, and the van fell behind. He adjusted his rear-view mirror when he noticed the passenger speaking into either a phone or walkie-talkie—he couldn't tell from such a distance.

When the exit fed into the main road, he turned right, and sure enough, the van followed suit, and soon it was beside him in the left lane.

Ron considered it a fit of paranoia, but he still gave in to the temptation to play Speed Test. Increase. Decrease. Increase again. The van matched him. He noticed the blond fellow in a black suit and shades seated on the passenger side occasionally glanced over. He rolled down his window. "I'm in a relationship. Thank you, very much," he shouted.

The passenger said something to the driver, then spoke into his walkie-talkie.

Ron took his cell phone from his pocket and switched it to Video mode. He hit RECORD and held it out the window. The passenger said something to the driver, and in an instant, the van decelerated and took the next side road.

"Weirdos!" Ron shouted, then pressed STOP before putting his phone away.

In a short while, he found himself surrounded in a cloud of red clay dust. He felt like a genie trapped inside a lamp, and soon he would burst out and say "Hi, John Fayman. I'm here to grant your wish to be famous again."

When the cloud cleared, the long, one-story farmhouse came into view. A split-rail fence lined the property, and before he came to a stop, a trio of barking hounds rushed out to greet him.

The front door opened, and a man stepped out. Ron squinted to see if it was indeed him. The man rolled up the sleeves of his button-down shirt and walked up the dirt driveway with a confident stride. He leaned forward, squinted right back at Ron, and straightened up again. The hounds ceased their barking and retreated to the long plank porch, where they settled down to laze in the morning sun.

When Ron felt it was safe, he rolled down his window. "Mister Fayman?"

"Can I help you?" John asked.

It was remarkable. The man appeared to be in good health and peak physical condition. Ron expected him to bear the haggard look of neglect common among celebrities who shy away from the spotlight, as if fame were a life-giving sun that nourished them to immortality and they were starving. Yet, here was this giant of the horror film industry, looking every bit as tough, attractive, and fit as he did thirty years prior. The chiseled jaw, the strong cheekbones—the man was a sculpture's dream.

Ron pushed the car door open and stepped out. "I'm Ron, with the Horr-Onto, Toronto's largest horror film convention."

John didn't seem impressed, and after his best spiel, Ron found himself standing in the same spot he started, sweating in the sun.

I'm dying, he thought. *Might as well dig a grave right here and lay down in it.* He knew the words were coming before they left John's mouth.

"I'm afraid I'll have to decline," said John.

"Aw man, I was really—"

"I hope you understand."

No, I don't. Why wouldn't you want to meet your biggest fans? Ron thought but instead said "I do. It's just we really wanted someone big like you to show up. You're an icon in the business, and a name like yours would really draw a great crowd."

"Truly, I'm flattered, but I've been out of the business for a good while now. I don't want to come off as hard-up for attention."

"You're a rock star in the horror world. *Brain Attack* is like *Tommy* or *The Wall*, eh? You don't have to make a hundred albums if the one you make is solid gold, and that's what you did with *Brain Attack*. You're a legend among your fans, including me."

"Honestly, I think I did more than one good film. Much better, too. But I get it; the film resonates with people. Still, I really won't be able to make it."

"I understand."

"I appreciate that."

"It's no problem. We just really wish you could have shown up."

The dogs rose from their rest and sat up on the porch. John glanced over his shoulder at them. "Yes, I know, but—"

Ron watched the dogs step off the porch. "Well, I guess I shouldn't keep harassing you."

"It's no problem. Really, it was an honor even to be considered. Thank you so much."

"You're welcome. I just—"

One of the dogs barked.

"I should probably get going," Ron said, keeping an eye on the dogs to gauge his safety. "But real quick, I was just wondering if you've kept up with other cast members?"

John's eyes rolled in anticipation of the question he knew was coming. Ron didn't notice the annoyed expression, his own (even after such a disappointment) was still so far beyond ecstatic just to be in the presence of a living legend.

"You know, like Dan Lewis?" Ron asked.

The dogs looked distracted, and after a moment, they wandered off toward some distant tree.

John's chest swelled with a held breath. "How do you know that name?

It's not listed on—"

"The end credits or IMDB? I know. Some hardcore fan tracked down his name through a few commercials he did. I suppose you're familiar with the rumors, or should I say, urban legend?"

"What's that?"

"That he died during the filming of *Brain Attack* through, you know, psychic powers."

John *humphed* through gritted teeth. "That so?"

"Yeah. Some people believe you actually killed him, made his head explode. That's why you both—"

"Both what?"

Gave up acting. Ron felt ashamed for nearly saying it. "Went into other fields."

"You mean, disappeared into obscurity?"

Ron forced a smile.

"Look… Ron, was it?" John asked, and continued upon Ron's nod. "I'm really not into the whole spotlight thing. I prefer to stay under the radar. I made my money, I'm comfortable. I don't need a thing. But Danny, I'm sure he would love to do your Coronado thing."

"Horr-Onto," Ron corrected him.

"Yeah. Danny loves that kind of stuff. In fact, I was talking to him the other day—" He watched Ron's eyes grow wide. "—and he was telling me he really wished he could get back into the game. And, who knows," he said, and tapped Ron on the chest with a finger. "Maybe *this* is the very thing that'll put him back in the spotlight."

Ron stood slack-jawed and speechless in fanboy amazement. John smiled and nodded, waiting for the moment to pass.

"Are you serious?" Ron asked.

"I can't promise anything. I'll give him a ring, talk to him, tell him about your con thing and have him call you."

Another moment of frozen-faced fanboy worship, then Ron shook out of it. "Oh," he said and retrieved a business card from his inside jacket pocket and pointed to each line. "Here. There's my name. Con-tact information. The website, the whole nine."

John looked at the card intently before stuffing it into his pants pocket.

"Wow. Thank you, Mister Fayman. You've been a great help," Ron said, about to extend a hand when he felt a wet trickle run from his nose and over his lip. "Dang sinuses," he said, and wiped his nose with a wrist, only to find it smeared in red.

He tasted the salt of his own blood. "I'm sorry. That never happens to me. Must be the heights. Thin air or something. How do you guys get used to it?"

"We adapt," said John. "Mind over matter."

"Well, I want to thank you for your time," Ron said, and extended a blood-streaked hand, which was refused. "I'm sorry you're not interested. It really would have been—"

Blood pulsed from his nose. "There it goes again," he said, and wiped his nose on his wrist and sleeve.

"You should probably be going," said John. "Before this thin air does some real damage."

"You're probably right. Thanks again for your time," Ron said with a wave.

"No problem," John said with the kind of disturbing, frozen smile a ventriloquist's dummy would wear.

Ron got in the car, pulled the seat belt strap over his shoulder, and straightened the rear-view mirror. In its reflection stood John, still wearing the dummy's smile as he waved farewell. A chill ran down Ron's spine and a dull pain throbbed in his left temple.

He put the car in gear and drove down the dirt road. In the mirror, he watched the man and house shrink before they disappeared behind the forest of maples. The pain shrunk, too, and soon was gone from his mind.

Chapter Four

Ron waited at the cemetery, the gravestones uncomfortably close. *An odd place to meet someone*, he thought. He was reminded of his earlier thought about digging graves and the disastrous meeting between him and John. At least something good had come out of it, though the something was certainly taking its sweet time, especially considering how quickly Dan Lewis had called him.

He looked at the clock on his cell phone: 2:46 p.m.—over thirty minutes late. His gaze wandered up the grassy hill along the dirt path leading to the concrete lot where his car was parked, only its grill and headlights visible from his vantage point. It had taken him five hours to reach Fayman's farm, another hour and a half to reach the cemetery, and still another four hours to get home.

He groaned, dreading the long ride. He thought of dialing back Dan, but the number was unlisted, and service was currently unavailable. As much as he wanted to leave, it was the opportunity of a life-time, and since he had his iPhone, he might as well take some pictures of the graveyard for the convention.

He walked through the crisp grass looking for unusual gravestones, especially any with figures: angels, gargoyles…anything would do. It was late enough in the day that the sun cast compelling shadows on the headstones and across the grave yard. With the proper angle or a little editing in post, he could hide the names of his unwitting extras, unsure whether or not the dead were even liable in such cases.

He snapped shot after shot. Name after name. He went further into the cemetery, and though the rows ran in straight lines north, south, east, and west, he felt as if he were spiraling deeper and deeper into the center of an inescapable maze. Stranger still, he felt as though he were being drawn into it against his will.

He turned back to locate his car. It was still there, atop the hill, though now much further away. He looked at the time on his phone again: 3:01 p.m.

"Damn it, Dan. Where are you?" he asked aloud.

He looked down at his feet. And there he was. Engraved into the stone:

DANIEL REGINALD LEWIS
1943–1981

Ron's jaw dropped open.

"Hell of a gimmick, huh?" a soft voice came from behind.

Ron turned around. Dan Lewis stood before him, arms crossed, left hand cradling his chin. Like John Fayman, the man had not aged. Thin, though fit, mustache still dark. Where he differed from John—the sculpture's dream—Dan was more like an artist's sketch: circle for a head, rectangular neck, oval chest; every bit of him could be illustrated with basic shapes.

Ron was amazed nonetheless, laughing in disbelief. "Mister Lewis. What's going on?"

"All part of Crane Owensby's surrealistic charm. Make his fans question reality or their sanity."

"*He* started the rumors?"

Dan smiled. A hand casually pointed at the grave, then returned to his chin. "And paid for the plot. He's not a revolutionary for nothing."

Ron shook his head. "Apparently not."

"So tell me about your convention."

Chapter Five

The two walked through the cemetery grounds, discussing issues of pay, accommodations, and all the little details until they came to a satisfactory agreement. Ron enjoyed every second of it, thoroughly captivated with Danny's presence. They were now on a first-name basis, though he felt it extremely difficult to say. In Ron's mind, the formerly nameless Head-Explode Guy was still very much "Mr. Lewis."

They had come full circle, arriving back where they started, when Dan stopped and doubled over as if sucker-punched in the gut. A hand shot to his temple, a grimace upon his face.

Ron gasped. "Mister Lewis! Danny. You alright?"

Dan looked over his shoulder, the hand on his temple now covering his eyes as if to shield them from the sun even though it was well behind them. He squinted, tried to focus.

Ron followed the direction of Dan's gaze, up the hillside to the lot where his and two other vehicles were parked. One was obviously Dan's.

The other was a white van.

"Friends of yours?" Ron asked.

"Friends? Sure, kid," said Dan, his voice much harsher. "They're my bodyguards. Keeping an eye on me to make sure you're not some crazed stalker."

Ron laughed, then felt quite embarrassed. "Me? No. I'm not a stalker."

"Easy, kid. I was only funning with you," Dan said, then massaged his temple again.

A trickle of blood ran down his nose. He wiped his hand and saw the blood.

"Oh, here you go," said Ron, reaching into his shirt pocket to retrieve some napkins. "Picked these up from the gas station. It's this crazy—"

"Mountain air? Yeah, I know," Dan finished his sentence and accepted the napkins. "Thanks, kid."

He wiped his nose. "Let me just give these guys the okay signal."

Dan stopped squinting, stood straight, and raised a hand, palm forward. A moment later, an engine started, and the van reversed down the hill with a screech of tires.

"Boy, you got them trained," Ron noted.

"You must learn to be assertive."

"I guess so."

"No, Ron. I'm telling you: *you* must learn to be assertive. Don't let people control you. Have a spine. Stand up for yourself. Learn to develop an iron will. Got it?"

Ron stood, speechless. He wasn't sure what warranted such a rebuke, or was it Dan's idea of encouragement? He swallowed and nodded.

Dan smiled. "Good," he said, placing a firm hand around Ron's shoulder. "Let's get out of here. This place is depressing."

The two followed the dirt path up the hillside to their vehicles.

Chapter Six

Ron took the flier from the printer and held it in both hands to examine it. He bent his arms to bring it closer in a faux zoom, then straightened his arms and leaned back for a wide-angle view. He cocked his head and blew through pursed lips. "Man. This'll never do."

The flier featured the side-by-side before-and-after photos of Dan's iconic scene, except the after-shot was a mess of motion blur. He laid the flier on his desk, picked up his cell phone, and called Franklin.

Ron pressed SPEAKER and placed the phone on his desk.

"Bonjour," came Franklin's voice.

"I need a favor," said Ron.

"What you got?"

"Can you do a BluRay screen-cap of the exploding head scene and email it to me? I used one from the DVD and wouldn't you know, it just plain sucks."

Franklin laughed, a non-linguistic I-told-you-so. "Yeah. I can handle that. Do you—"

Ron's suddenly straightened up as a thought hit him. "Oh wait. Actually, can you do a before-and-after, like the shot a few frames back? I can't have two different resolutions on the same flier. That would look bad."

"You mean the frame with the dummy? I wouldn't do that. I mean, it's a damn-convincing dummy, but it's still a dummy."

Ron considered Franklin's words, then said, "Nah. Get the one of him where he's smiling all cocky and arrogant. Can you do that?"

"Yeah. No problem. Get it to you by tonight."

"Cool. Thank you."

"You're welcome. You out?" Franklin asked.

"I'm out," said Ron.

"Au revoir."

Ron ended the call.

A few hours later Ron held the much-improved flier in hand. "Ah, perfection."

He returned to the monitor and clicked the #Copies icon, entered 500 on his keyboard, and clicked PRINT. A few minutes later, the dizzying smell of toner filled the room and he had 500 copies of the Horr-Onto flier.

Chapter Seven

With clear skies and a promise of front-of-the-line passes, Franklin convinced a handful of future con-goers to hand fliers out to every male and female in a t-shirt, regardless of age.

The three young men and two ladies canvased the neighborhood surrounding Queen Street West, ducking into coffee shops and shisha bars in search of horror-hogs and gore-hounds, and just perhaps a chance to rest their feet.

Quinn had just exited the shisha bar, the scent of smoky mint clinging to her green mackinaw and platinum hair peeking out her matching tuque. Perhaps she was a little too relaxed, as she forgot her present demographic and began shoving fliers at every person she passed, wearing a smile that was entirely too large.

One elderly lady said no. Her friend took the flier and immediately gasped at its graphic image. She handed it back, but Quinn had already wandered off, so she found the nearest recycling bin to discard the distasteful flier.

Quinn stopped at the corner of an intersection and waited for the crosswalk light. The bus pulled to the curb and stopped to discharge its passengers onto the sidewalk. She turned to see the emerging crowd and shoved a flier at the first man to exit.

"What's this?" the barely-silver senior asked.

"The Horr-Onto: Toronto's largest horror convention."

"Yes. I've heard of it," he said, annoyed, then jammed a finger at the exploding head of Dan Lewis. "I mean *this*. Why do you have his picture on here?"

"It's from *Brain Attack*. It's only the coolest movie ever."

The man walked off, highly agitated. Quinn shrugged and continued shoving fliers at the others on the corner.

Crane Owensby clutched the flier with white knuckles as he made his way up the sidewalk, grumbling to himself. "Stupid know-nothing. I made the damn movie."

Chapter Eight

Crane stared at the flier lying on his desk with utter contempt; his fingers drummed the oak surface while he mentally weighed his options.

He spun counterclockwise in his swivel chair and watched the movie posters on his wall roll past like a time machine stopping at the milestones of his film career: *nTerfacE*—his venture into the addictive world of computer gaming; *BetaMaximus*—his sister venture into the home video craze of the '80s; *The Tingler*—a body horror remake of the Vincent Price classic; and finally but firstly, the film that put him on the proverbial map and secured his place in the annals of cult filmdom—Brain Attack.

He paused in his chair and sighed. "Why can't I bury you already? What's it gonna take?"

He stared at the illustrated image of Dan Lewis' exploding head. He felt the blood rushing through his arteries into his own head and gritted his teeth. With a final kick, he came full circle in his swivel chair, back before his desk, the flier, the bio-mech typewriter designed by H.R. Giger for his film adaption of Franz Kafka's *Metamorphosis*, and the telephone that seemed to grow before his eyes.

He picked up the handset and dialed the phone number on the keypad.

A click, then a muffled male voice came through the tiny speaker. "Hello?"

"It's Crane," the writer-director announced.

"I suspected you'd call."

Crane took the flier from the desk. His tight grip creased through the paper. "I am presently holding in my hand a flier for the upcoming Horr-Onto Con. I don't suppose I have to tell you what's on it."

A soft cough. "No, I've seen it."

"I also suppose I don't have to tell you I'm none too happy about it?"

"That's understandable."

"You know any such appearance at this convention is a serious breach of contract?"

A sigh. "Yes, I understand that."

Crane placed the flier on the table and retrieved a pen from a cylindrical holder, which he drummed and twirled in the air. "I'm glad you do. So the question is, at this critical juncture we presently find ourselves at, what are you going to do about it?"

"That's my business."

Crane leaned forward. "Is that so?"

"That's so. It's none of your concern."

Crane ground his back teeth as he sketched a pair of angular horns upon the yet-destroyed version of Dan Lewis's image. "I think it is, and if you don't do something, I will, and it won't be pretty, I can guarantee you that."

Crane scribbled a series of lines over Dan's face—first vertical, then horizontal, then a shrinking spiral—until the face was consumed in a ball of black ink.

"Look, you do what you have to do. Let me do what I have to do. Okay?" the voice spoke.

"We had a contract," said Crane. "It's been breached. So all bets are off."

"Quit bitching. The contract is still in effect. Consider it taken care of."

Crane snatched the defiled flier up. "Would I be holding a flyer that says 'Special Guest Dan Lewis,' if it was?"

Another sigh, followed by an exasperated tone. "There won't be any appearance."

Crane cradled the headset between head and shoulder. "I'm supposed to take your word for it? No, I'll be there to make sure."

"If you show up at that convention and make a scene, you'll regret it."

"I only regret trusting you to keep your end of the bargain," said Crane as he crumpled the flier into a ball.

"I'm warning you, Crane. Don't get in my way."

"You seem to forget I have connections, too."

A chuckle. The phone clicked in Crane's ear.

He slammed the handset to the receiver and swiveled in his chair until he faced the metal mesh recycle bin in the corner of the room. He tossed the flier into the bin.

Chapter Nine

The Tiger Lotus-Toronto Convention Center & Hotel was abuzz with over a thousand anxious fans, several in full costume and make-up honoring their favorite villains, victims, and heroes. Actors great and small manned their tables, signing autographs, shaking hands, or taking pictures with the faithful.

Ron stood in the center of the lobby and spun around to take in the panorama of booths advertising their features and familiar faces associated with them. From up-and-coming to heavy-hitters, names like Nevermore Production Films, Red Headed Revolution, Jet-Powered Films, Full Moon, Troma, DarkSky, and Ghosthouse flashed by.

It was every bit as exciting as sitting front and center before the wide-screen, eating stale over-buttered-and-salted popcorn, watching your favorite horror film on replay. Like a time-lapsed video, he watched the lines thin and reform into one long, single line from one end of the enormous lobby to the other, and with time, that new, unified line shrunk as the auditorium filled to near capacity.

A beep on his cell phone brought him back to the present. He glanced at the time: 2:45 p.m.

He unclipped the walkie-talkie from his hip and pressed TALK. "Gorehound Two, this is Gorehound One, come in. Over." He released the button and waited.

A blip. "Gorehound One, this is Gorehound Two. Over," Franklin's distorted voice came in.

"We have fifteen minutes till go-time. Over."

"Roger that. Target is in place and ready to blow your mind. Over."

Ron laughed. Adrenaline shot through his veins. His stomach swirled with anticipation. "Roger that. Over."

He shook his head in disbelief and lowered the walkie-talkie to his hip, then brought it quickly to his lips and pressed TALK. "Despite all the bumps in the road, we did it, buddy. And like always, I couldn't have done any of this without you. Thanks, Frank."

He released the button and waited.

A chuckle came over the speaker. "Bienvenue. First round is on you."

Ron shook his head again. "You got it, brother. My pleasure. See you in five."

"Roger that. Over."

Ron made his way across the near-empty lobby, admiring the long, rectangular fountain of floating flowers. Far off, before the auditorium door, two blond men in dark blue jackets, black slacks, shoes, and shades stood before the sandy-haired genius himself.

"So you showed up after all," said Crane.

"I was about to say the same thing," said the man on the right.

"The difference is I said I would."

"I never said I wouldn't."

With a thumb, Crane pointed over his shoulder at the grooved letter board standing behind him. Plastic white letters against the black background read:

3 PM to 4 PM......DANIEL LEWIS

Actor of Television and Cinema,

The Interrogator from

Crane Owensby's Cult Classic

BRAIN ATTACK

"Yet look who's about to go on," said Crane. "I thought you said there would be no appearance."

"I'm aware of the problem."

"Yet you did nothing about it."

"I'll handle it."

"Handle it how? Are you going to politely ask him to walk off stage?"

The man pulled back his jacket to reveal a gun. "I'm prepared to use force if necessary."

"It *will* be necessary—*now*. Had you taken care of this before, there wouldn't be any reason for this."

"Quit bitching," the man said, and pointed to the lapel radio on his shoulder. "All I have to do is press this button and backup comes running."

"I hope they're fast on their feet and have one hell of an aim. If he has time to achieve Gamma, you can all kiss your asses goodbye," Crane's voice cracked. He massaged his temples with his thumb and middle finger. "We all can. God help us."

The two men in suits eyed the approaching fan.

"Oh man!" said Ron, his face illuminated with reverence in the presence of his idol. "Crane Owensby?! You came to *our* convention?"

Crane clenched his jaws and looked away. "Can you take care of this?" he asked, then entered the auditorium.

"Just a minute of your time," Ron said, about to step into the auditorium before the door shut when a hand pulled him back by the collar.

He turned around and raised a finger. "Hands off!" he snapped. "I'm not some fanboy. I'm running this show. And who put you guys in charge? You're not my security."

He reached for his walkie. "Secur—"

The man on the left snatched the walkie from his hand.

"Hey!" Ron protested.

"Your Security is now under our jurisdiction," said the man on the right as he flashed a wallet with badge and ID.

Ron remembered Dan's rebuke. He straightened up and puffed his chest out. "I don't care who you clowns are. You're not on my payroll. Understood?"

In an instant, the man pulled a pistol from his hip holster and shoved it in Ron's nose.

Ron's hands shot up in surrender and his voice half an octave. "Don't shoot me!"

"Listen here, fanboy. If you weren't so damned stuck on your bromance, I wouldn't be here. You don't know what you've done. You've put every one of these lives at risk, not to mention mine and your own. Not that I give a rat's ass about yours at this point."

The armed man turned to his partner. Ron's eyes followed. "Gary, will you see our friend here outside?" said the man. "Maybe we can save at least one life."

"What about the other fellow?" Gary asked.

Ron's eyes shot back to the man holding the gun up his nose. "You mean Frank? He's my partner."

The man didn't face Ron as he shook his head. "Too late for him."

Gary put an iron grip on Ron's arm and roughly escorted him toward the lobby's entrance. Though relieved the gun was no longer up his nose, Ron kept his hands up, looked back, and shouted his concerns at the man. "What do you mean, too late? What's going on here?"

The dozen or so fans in lines of various B-actors' tables turned to see the reason for Ron's outburst.

"Don't make a scene," Gary mumbled, his left hand reaching into his jacket to reveal his pistol.

Ron's eyes widened. "Jesus Murphy. Why is everybody flashing guns?"

They exited the building. About 20 meters from the hotel sat a familiar white van.

"Hey. I know that van," said Ron. "You're Danny's bodyguards, aren't you? Didn't he give you the all-clear? He said you guys wouldn't bother me after the other day. Remember? At the cemetery?"

"I remember it well," Gary said, stopping in his tracks to face Ron.

He pulled down his shades. His left eye was milky white, only the hint of an iris remaining.

"Your 'friend' Danny did this. Only he's not your friend—and he certainly isn't Danny."

"What are you talking—"

Gary pushed his shades back up his nose and jerked Ron by the arm and continued to the van. A man ran across the parking lot left to right with a line of yellow police tape, cutting off the Center and everyone inside.

"What's he doing?" Ron asked.

Before any answer came, police and military vehicles pulled up behind the line, lights flashing, sirens silent. Doors swung open and officers and soldiers in full gear stepped out, their guns drawn.

Looking over his shoulder, Ron watched attendees exit the lobby. Some soldiers ran toward the evacuees. Under gunpoint, they were told to raise their hands and close their eyes. Ron thought it an odd command to shout at someone.

A moment later, a woman in a white lab coat was escorted by soldiers to the restrained group. One by one, she waved a metal wand on both sides of their heads and offered a nod. The attendees were then escorted to their vehicles and asked to leave. If they didn't wish to leave, they were advised to stay at a safe distance behind the yellow police line.

"What are you guys doing?" Ron asked.

When he faced Gary, he realized they were at the van. Gary pulled the handle on the side door and slid it open. Inside sat a veritable control room of flashing lights, switches, screens, and surveillance equipment, all on metal paneling painted gray.

Two pairs of headphones hung on hooks, their fat, curling wires leading to input jacks on a vertical panel. A mounted microphone sat between them on the connecting horizontal panel.

One particular box caught Ron's attention. Like all the equipment, it was gray metal. A circular green screen, similar to an oscilloscope, displayed a relatively flat but animated line of significantly lighter green. Beneath the screen sat a dial. The angled positions surrounding it read clockwise, left to right: Delta, Theta, Alpha, Beta, Gamma.

Ron gasped. He pointed at the box with his free hand. "That's the machine from *Brain Attack*."

"Wrong again. The machine in *Brain Attack* is from us. Unfortunately, we're too far out of range for it to work."

Ron faced his captor. "Psi-Corp is real?"

"Only the names have been changed to protect the guilty. Get inside."

Ron was paralyzed with fear.

"Move it," Gary ordered, and shoved him into the van, then climbed in behind him.

Gary pulled the door shut. "Let's hope we're safe at this distance. And pray my partner makes it out alive," he said, pulling back his jacket to remind Ron of his pistol. "For your sake."

Ron swallowed hard.

Chapter Ten

Inside the auditorium, Dan Lewis commanded the stage like a proud peacock, a rooster among hens, even with his meek kids' show-host voice. He pointed to someone in the front row and spoke into his wireless handheld microphone. "Yes, you. In the purple tee-shirt."

Franklin hurried down the aisle with a second microphone. The unkempt fellow looked down at his shirt, then to his left and right and mouthed "Me?"

Dan nodded. "Yes, you. Go ahead."

Franklin reached him and held the microphone toward his mouth. The fellow touched the mic. When the scraping, swishing of his fingers sounded across the auditorium, he quickly pulled his hand back and cautiously leaned forward, pulled back, then leaned forward again, afraid his lips would brush the large windscreen.

"Thank you. First off, I want to say: huge fan, obviously, as all of us are."

A few whoops and hollers emboldened the nervous man, a new-found smile of confidence spreading across his face.

"I just wondered if you were aware of the rumors of your death, and if they were greatly exaggerated or not."

Laughs and brief applause sounded across the room, and when it sub-sided, he sat down.

Frank glanced at him and smiled. "Good question," he whispered, his hand over the mic.

Dan laughed. "Well, now, of course, that's just silly. I mean, here I am, in the flesh. Now, if I were to say, transform before your eyes into John Fayman, would that impress you?"

The fellow glanced to his left at Franklin and shrugged.

"You heard correctly. If I were to transform into John Fayman here and now, would that impress you?"

"Sure," the fellow said, but it went unheard until Franklin held the microphone to his mouth. "Sure," his voice boomed as he repeated him-self.

"Now, of course, it's a ridiculous statement. After all, it's impos-sible. Right?" said Dan, emphasizing his soft speech with louder hand gestures. "I mean, even with today's most spectacular CGI, you can still tell, ninety-nine percent of the time, what is real and what isn't. No ... Special effects just aren't what they used to be. Then again," he laughed to himself, "they were sometimes stupidly simple.

"For example, the scene where John Fayman wants to sneak past the Psi-Corp guards, so he transforms into one of them. Of course, he didn't really transform, neither onscreen or offscreen. It was all camera edits. He stood in a spot marked on the floor, with the tripod-mounted camera facing him. They took the shot, called cut, then Jimmy Beck, the actor who portrayed the guard, stepped onto the same spot, and they filmed the next shot. Stupidly simple, but effective.

"In the viewer's mind, he transformed, but it was nothing more than a bait and switch with video edits. Now, if I were to cease looking like myself, let's say, and instantly become John Fayman, would you believe all along I was John Fayman or Danny Lewis? Who knows? But just as an experiment, let's see what happens."

Half the audience was busy glancing at one another when gasps of awe drew their eyes back to the stage, where true to his word, Dan Lewis had changed, in the blink of an eye, to John Fayman. Eyes squinted, were rubbed; glasses were removed and wiped clean of offending spots, then replaced, but the image remained: John Fayman stood on the stage, mic in hand.

The clothes stayed the same, the position of every limb, but the face, build, height, weight—no matter how different or similar—were changed. Where smooth, bare arms extended past rolled-up sleeves, now rippled muscle lay beneath a thick coat of hair.

Franklin unclipped his walkie-talkie and pressed TALK. "Gore-hound One, this is Gorehound Two. Come in. Over," he whispered into the mouthpiece.

He waited a moment. "Gorehound One. Are you seeing this?"

Silence.

"Gorehound One. Where are you?"

When no answer came, he clipped the two-way radio back to his belt and stared in disbelief with the rest of the audience.

"Now, relax," said John in his signature gravel-like voice, drastically different than Dan's soft, soothing timbre. "That was nothing big. I mean, when you consider the power of the human mind, you could simply tell yourself it was all power of suggestion. Mass hypnosis.

"After all, the fliers and online ads said Danny Lewis would be here, so perhaps your mind superimposed his likeness over my own. And when you think about it, we're not all that different looking: two white guys, both bald, both sport mustaches on occasion. An easy mistake. You thought I was Danny, I get it.

John (or was it still Dan?) stopped his casual pacing and sighed. He gazed up at the high, hot lights bearing down on him. He wiped a stinging tear from his eye.

"Daniel Reginald Lewis was my friend. We roomed together for years before we got into the industry. We busted our asses working every crappy part-time job we could find just to survive while pursuing our dream to be movie stars. He was doing commercials. I was cast in horror and sci-fi flicks. Then finally, our big break came.

"Crane Owensby opened up the heavens and smiled upon us, and said, 'These are my only begotten sons, and I'm going to screw them up permanently'."

He pointed into the audience, his eyes scanning its depths. "You hear me, Crane? Yes, I know you're out there. I can hear your sniveling thoughts even now. Don't worry. You'll get what you came for."

From Stage Right, the man in a dark blue jacket and black shades appeared. Audience members held their cell phones high, recording the events. Their voices stirred throughout the room, no one sure what was taking place.

John glanced away, then held the mic close to his lips. "I'm sorry. Where was I? Oh yes. Ladies and gentlemen, may I introduce, Agent Edwards," he said, and with a sweeping motion, pointed to Stage Right.

An unsure few applauded until the man opened his jacket and drew his gun.

Franklin walked toward the emergency exit, the legs of his crisp khakis loudly swishing, the walkie-talkie to his lips. "Security? We have an emergency. On stage pronto!"

He thrust open the door and glanced back, expecting the audience to come rushing out, half-wondering how he had not already been trampled in such a mass exit, but not a soul moved. A hand jerked him by the collar and pulled him from the door, letting it slam shut.

The soldier held a raised rifle. "Hands up! Close your eyes!" he ordered.

"What?" Franklin asked.

"Close your eyes or I put a bullet between them!"

"Okay!" Franklin squealed, shutting his eyes so tight they hurt.

He heard a blip, much like the walkie-talkie he sported.

"Target Three has just exited the building, rear point of entry," said the soldier.

"What do you mean, Target Three?" Franklin asked.

"Shut up!" the soldier ordered.

Franklin's heart raced. His breathing soon caught up. Footsteps sounded. He tried to breathe shallowly to hear what was going on. It must have been a dozen men. Or was it a dozen feet? That would mean six men. Franklin's thoughts now raced as fast as his heart.

"What's your name?" a new voice spoke, female.

"Franklin St. Ange."

Franklin felt the cool of metal by his right ear. A gun? "Oh God, don't shoot me! Please!"

"Relax," said the woman.

You try relaxing with a gun to your head, he thought.

A hum sounded in his right ear, followed by an inexplicable ticking in the center of his head, somewhere inside his skull.

"Tell me how you feel, right now," said the woman.

Tick. Tick. Tick tick. Tick. Tick tick tick.

"Scared. Terrified. About to piss my pants. Why is my head ticking?" said Franklin.

The cool feeling abated. So did the hum and the ticking. He exhaled, but too soon. The cool feeling came to the left of his head. Then the hum. And the ticking. He gasped. His ears stopped up. He swallowed. They popped.

"Would you like to kill me?" the woman asked.

Franklin shook his head, confused. "What? Kill you? I don't even know you."

There was a pause. The hum and the cool feeling passed. But the ticking remained. The cool humming returned.

"Would you kill me if you had the chance?" she asked.

Franklin shook his head. "No. Why would I?"

The cool humming passed. Then returned. The ticking stopped. The cool humming continued, then left.

"He's clear," she said.

Footsteps sounded and soon began to fade.

"You can look now," said the soldier.

Franklin opened his eyes. He saw a woman in a white lab coat walking off, her dark hair pinned in a bun and a fat metal wand in her hand. The entourage of soldiers surrounding her escorted her out of sight.

"Come with me," said the soldier, his hand on Franklin's back to prod him onward.

With both hands on his rifle, the soldier led Franklin around the building and proceeded toward a white van parked behind a line of police tape.

Chapter Eleven

"Yes, friends," said John before his attentive audience. "The hour of my betrayal is at hand. And he's followed by a Canadian legion not close behind, no doubt. All lackeys from the Ministry of Psy-Ops, the organization you know better as Psi-Corp."

"John Fayman, I need you to come with me," said Agent Edwards.

John faced him. "Not a chance in Hell."

Agent Edwards raised his gun. "John Fayman, I repeat. I need you to come with me. Do not resist."

John waved a finger in window wiper fashion. "Ah ah ah." His stare intensified.

Agent Edwards froze, noticeably so. His grimace and darting eyes cried for help. The audience gasped.

John looked aside to the audience. "Listen, friends, the real conspiracy is not that I killed Danny Lewis, my best friend, unintentionally at Owensby's brutal direction, or that I was forced into silence and seclusion afterwards, but this: after the Canadian authorities investigated Danny's death and confiscated *Brain Attack*'s original footage, they discovered my blossoming power.

"They took over production of the film and further enlisted Crane Owensby, a man who doesn't possess an ounce of psychic will, to produce a series of training films for their psychic boot camp using his viewers as test subjects. You know them as the other two-thirds of the *Mind Trilogy*: *BetaMaximus* and *nTerfacE*.

"*His viewers*," John said, waving a finger toward the audience. "That means *you*. Like it or not, you've been trained and conditioned as the world's premiere psychic army. How do you like that? Do you recall an invitation to enlist? Too bad. You were drafted. Dragged out of your peaceful, pacifist childhood by a government hell-bent on war.

"Why? As a deterrent to the psychic soldiers produced by Russia and the United States. Done without your consent so that when the time arises—that is, when a sufficient enemy of Canada has been fabricated and erected through the Ministry of Propaganda and Misinformation— you will be willing to kill solely with the power of your mind.

"If you think I'm making this up, then ask yourself why Agent Edwards has a gun pointed at me right now, yet is powerless to move a muscle."

A shout came from the audience. "It's part of the show!"

Weak applause and uneasy laughter followed.

John scanned the audience until he found the smirking young man high-fiving his friend in the seat next to him. John smiled a sinister smile, not unlike his character Jarred Galway would wear.

"Yes, it's all part of the show. Excuse me. What's your name, son?" he asked.

The young fellow yelled his name, but it was lost in the continuing applause.

"I'm sorry. I didn't hear you," said John, motioning for the audience to quiet. They gradually obliged. "Frank? Where are you?"

"He left!" someone shouted.

With a sigh of acceptance, John nodded. "We don't have a microphone, so you'll have to speak louder."

"Terry," the fellow shouted.

"Thank you, Terry. Now if you would, Terry, would you mind taking that pen you were hoping to get my autograph with and jab it into your own eyes?"

Terry's smile disappeared, then flashed again, the muscles of his face twitching with uncertainty. He glanced to his friend, who gave him just as uncertain a shrug. Terry laughed nervously.

"You see, friends," John said, raising a finger. "Terry *does* mind. That's why he's having a bit of trouble deciding if he should obey me or not. With that said, I have to be a bit more direct. That's how brain attacking works. I could simply think it, but in this case, so that you may know the son of man has power on earth to harm the living: Terry, take that pen and jab it into both your eyes."

Terry laughed again, yet his fingers twirled the pen upside down and closed upon it in a tight fist. His friend laughed, jabbed him in the arm with an elbow, yet Terry raised the pen, his laughter turning into panicked breathing, then loud whimpers.

His friend continued laughing, which humored John enough to chuckle right along with him.

"Stop me, Evan," said Terry, the pen now at eye-level, his hand trembling, the other gripped tight around his wrist.

Evan laughed.

"I'm serious, man. Stop me."

The pen approached his right eye.

The audience before him had spun around to watch, those behind him leaned forward to the edge of their seats. Cell phone cameras and anxious faces surrounded him.

"I'm not kidding. He's making me do this. Please, I'm begging you! Somebody stop me!"

"Come on, man, cut it out," said Evan, but it was too late.

With a scream, the pen pierced Terry's eyeball, shooting out a jet of milky fluid. A clear jelly squirted out and ran down his cheek. Evan grabbed at his wrists and wrestled the pen from him, pulling out a portion of the gooey, deflated ball with it.

The audience applauded.

A fellow seated immediately in front of them smiled and nodded repeatedly. "Awesome!"

"It's not a trick, man!" Evan shouted in his face. "Somebody call an ambulance! This is real!"

"He's right," said John. "That was real. No special effects. And to Terry, and your friend, I'm sorry I had to do that. But you see, it's time for those of you with the power and fortitude to arise. The doubters, like dear Terry there, will quickly fall by the wayside and be eaten by the birds. That's what the government wants: faithful assassins or dubious drones. Terry would have been the latter."

Evan pulled his cell phone from his pocket and dialed the number for the police, the audience roaring all the while. He eyed the phone's screen: SERVICE UNAVAILABLE.

Chapter Twelve

"What are you doing?" Franklin asked, cramped inside the van with Ron and Gary.

"Blocking all communications," Gary answered. "We suspect Fayman can not only hack minds, but devices. Any signal coming or going is a point of escape or attack if he so chooses."

Chapter Thirteen

John clasped his hands with a sharp clap. It echoed through the high-ceilinged auditorium. "So now the real question is: are you a true fan of *Brain Attack*?"

The crowd applauded.

"What do you say we show Agent Edwards a little pyrokinetic hospitality?"

Roars rose from the audience.

"Just focus all your rage upon him. Think how the government was willing to use you to kill someone you've never met, someone who's never done you a bit of wrong. Think how Agent Edwards here would be more than happy to put you on the front line in harm's way to fight a rich man's war. Now use that rage like a magnifying glass."

"Stop it, Fayman! Stop it!" a shout boomed over the loudspeaker.

Eyes gazed up and around, searching for the mighty Wizard behind the curtain.

With a jerk of his head and a savage growl, John shifted his gaze to the glass-shielded sound booth. Behind the silver-tinted window, an obscured shape ducked out of sight. At John's gaze, the window vibrated and rattled.

An explosion of glass rained down upon those at the rear of the auditorium. They covered their heads and screamed.

"Crane! I knew you couldn't hide for long!" said John. "Why don't you come out here and take your medicine like a man?"

With John's power redirected, a phased Agent Edwards was finally able to move and squeezed off a shot. He was aiming for the heart, but John's left shoulder took the bullet, evidenced by the blossoming flower dying his shirt red. He spun back toward the agent and froze him again where he stood.

Now John's eyes flicked side to side, his focus masterfully divided between two potentially fatal foes: the one standing before him with gun raised, the other burrowed into his shoulder an inch from his heart.

A sucking sound preceded a spray of blood that shot out from his shoulder like a shaken soda can popped open as a prank. Amid the bubbling, bloody red fizz emerged the deformed bullet that had sunk inside his flesh. It spun like a screw in reverse, working its way out, and fell onto the hardwood stage, rolling, rattling.

A tendril of smoke rose from the bullet hole in his shirt as he cauterized his wound at will. John smiled and returned his full attention once more to Agent Edwards. "What do you think? Would you like a smoke?"

Two blurry, white dots appeared on the agent, then converged into a smaller, brighter dot. It began to burn.

"Join me, friends," said John. "Imagine Agent Edwards being the size of an ant beneath the beautiful, blazing, burning sun of your omnipotent, all-powerful being, your brain, your mind!"

Already the white dots were forming. Intense stares fell upon the frozen agent from the angry audience.

Another gunshot.

A red dot appeared on John Fayman's head. His beautiful, terrifying brain was pierced by a bullet on one end and left the other side of his head out a hole twenty times larger. He collapsed onto the stage.

Smoke plumed from the muzzle of Crane Owensby's pistol. Several in the audience gazed at their fallen hero, then back at the booth. Others—the truly harmful others—were already locked in a lethal state of meditation, and nothing, absolutely nothing, would deter them now.

Crane exited the booth and fled for the lobby, ready to shoot anyone who looked at him the wrong way—the deathly, deadly, fatal way.

Some rose to their feet and pursued, not to harm him, but to escape the madness taking over the audience.

"Leave me alone! I had to do it!" he shouted, firing into the panicked crowd.

A stray bullet struck a girl in the chest, throwing her back into the fleeing fans before they turned or dropped to the floor.

Crane reached the double-door entrance. He leaned his shoulder into it the door as his hands hit the push bar and stumbled out onto the lobby floor. Lying on his back, he looked into the auditorium as the door slowly swung shut. He gazed at the nightmare he helped create: the Ministry of Psy-Ops' elite force of psychic soldiers.

The door closed.

The audience focused the entirety of their hatred upon Agent Edwards. It continued to manifest as a series of white dots upon his suit and flesh. Searing, white-hot hatred.

Smoke appeared on a sleeve, then a breast pocket; a curling, wispy thing that would float just above the fire-red end of a cigarette.

The stage mic picked up the singeing sound of clothes as they gave way to tiny tongues of fire. Agent Edwards tried to flee from their burning gazes, but his feet were frozen to the stage. He swung his arms about to pull himself free as if stuck in knee-deep quicksand, but he only managed to knock over the microphone, which landed with a loud crash and momentary ear-piercing feedback.

The puddle of blood from John's pulpy, empty head pooled beneath the microphone and shorted it out with brilliant, popping sparks.

The white spots on Agent Edwards's face and hands, instead of igniting into flame, simply sunk into his flesh as if it were soft wax, sizzling and burrowing like flaming worms through muscle until they came to bone. He screamed in agony, and within a moment, he lit up like a torch.

Papery ash that had been his jacket fell from his flailing arms as he twisted the trunk of his body in a grotesque dance. Now that the flaming darts of thought had hit their mark, the power that had held his feet frozen to the floor relented.

The captive was released to stumble across the stage like a drunkard, a firefly flitting to and fro until its wings were no more than a wiry frame. When he finally collapsed to the floor, he strangely resembled a campfire, one set ablaze for the audience's amusement.

Outside in the lobby, Crane curled into a ball, his head tucked beneath his knees, and covered his ears with his arms. He tried to block out the awful din, but it wasn't an audible noise. It was inside him, in his head, so loud his own terrified thoughts faded to a faint whisper, then nothing.

All he heard were the thoughts of some thousands of fans just beyond the wall behind him; their fiery, brain-melting, all-consuming thoughts bent on conquest. The whole of mankind would be at their mercy. No one was safe.

GRAVE MARKER

ANDREW RICHARDSON

THE
BATHTUB

Chapter One

"After you, my English Rose."

"Thank you. You're a gentleman, as always." Lizzie stepped through Paolo's doorway and paused to admire his flat while Paolo and Brad followed. "It's just as I'd expect from a suave Italian banker—plush and posh." She breathed in slowly. "And subtle potpourri; not overwhelming. You certainly know how to welcome a girl."

Brad winked. "Paolo's bathroom is even better," he said in the Australian twang as thick as his broad shoulders.

Lizzie's cheeks warmed. After taking in the thick burgundy carpet, she pushed a strand of blond hair from her face so her gaze could rest on the leather furniture complementing the carpet and matching wallpaper. She slipped off her shoes, letting the thick pile caress her soles. "Lovely," she said.

"Only the best for our favorite soon-to-be-ex colleague." Paolo slipped off his suit jacket and hung it on a hook, leaving him in his crisp, white shirt. His deep brown eyes rolled over Lizzie like the gentle caresses she anticipated later. He said, "Would you like to see the bathroom now or wait until we've relaxed a bit?"

Lizzie's cheeks warmed some more.

"We're embarrassing the poor girl." Brad put a protective hand on hers, gently and for a moment longer than he needed to, giving Lizzie a chance to enjoy the reassurance of his touch. He hung his jacket next to Paolo's, letting his slightly tight shirt outline the torso Lizzie thought more suited to Bondi Beach than in an English bank. She licked a lip as she imagined him in only skimpy trunks, with the sun glistening off his surf-sodden body and the Pacific plastering his light brown mop to his head...

"My dear?" Paolo asked.

"I'm sorry. I was miles away." *On Bondi Beach.* She hung her own jacket over Brad's and wondered whether her lace bra was obvious beneath her blouse. *I hope so.*

Paolo flicked the coffee maker. It burst into a gurgle, sending the aroma of expensive beans into Lizzie's nostrils. She took in the room's scents while contrasting Paolo's suave Mediterranean looks and designer stubble with Brad's rugged and muscular physique.

"Lizzie, when you suggested this, I think it sounded like fun. But now we're here..." Brad shrugged. "We won't think any less of you if you decide to leave." He met her gaze and quickly looked away, as if begging her not to back out.

Lizzie spread her arms. "What sort of girl would I be if I let down my two hunkiest soon-to-be-ex colleagues? Especially as I can't stop thinking about it."

"I'm a little disappointed," Paolo said. "I'd hope you're fantasizing about it, not just thinking."

"Yes. Fantasizing. That's what I meant." Lizzie strode to Brad and put her arms around his neck. "Tomorrow I'll be starting my new life on the other side of the country waiting for my divorce to come through, so this is my best ever chance to live out my bathtub fantasy." She cocked her head. "There won't be any comeback, will there?"

Brad's uncertain grin became confident. "Not from me. And it'll address one of my fantasies, too."

Lizzie raised a brow. "Which one is that?"

The uncertainty returned to his smile. He pushed his mop of hair from his eyes. "The fantasy of wondering what my most stunning colleague wears beneath the navy skirt I see her in every day."

"What do you imagine me wearing?"

"Would it offend you if I said I think I've probably thought about you in every possible type and color?"

The flirting had Lizzie's heart pattering. "I'm flattered. I hope tonight's don't disappoint."

"You've no need to worry there. You'll look gorgeous whatever you've chosen." Paolo placed three china cups and saucers on the coffee table, then poured three brandies.

"I need one of those after my day," Brad said.

"We've been in a wine bar all evening," Paolo said. "Surely you don't need more."

"We've both been interviewed for that promotion. Don't you feel a little stressed out?" Brad asked.

"No, I'm laid back. May the best person get it." Paolo held out a hand. "Since my heart scare, I decided life's too short for stuff to get in the way."

The handshake between the men was genuine. *Like between me and Brad, when we both went for that job he got.*

"Yes, the best man." Brad tutted. "Then we had that ridiculous Cassandra woman in, demanding yet another loan. She's mad. After her ranting, I could empty an entire brewery."

"That's why I authorized a hundred pounds," Paolo said. "It was worth it to stop her making a scene in front of other customers. *Puttana.*" *Bitch.* His favorite insult finished the sentence.

The men looked at each other in silence. Brad's unspoken, *If I get the promotion she'll have no more loans...* hung stiffly in the air. He said, "Her ranting stressed me more than the interview, especially when she screamed about all bankers being immoral pigs."

"Hopefully Lizzie can unstress you," Paolo said.

"No pressure, then." Lizzie gave a nervous laugh. "The coffee smells wonderful."

"It's my favorite and tastes as good as it smells. I have it flown in from Italy. Take your time to enjoy it, we've got all evening." Paolo's hand rested on her wrist. He looked straight at her with the deep, brown eyes Lizzie wanted to fall into. "Indeed, we have all night."

Brad looked at his watch.

"It looks as if Brad's in a hurry," Lizzie said.

The Australian flushed. "No, I just wondered what the time was, that's all."

"Maybe you just want to back out," Lizzie teased.

"God, no. I'm fine."

"I'm fine, too, my English Rose. In fact, my dear, let me show you how fine I am." Paolo stood behind Lizzie. His arms slipped around her waist, gently pulling her to him and molding his torso against her back.

She caught a whiff of aftershave mingling with room's smells and the aroma of testosterone-laced sweat. Her hand touched his. "You two smell gorgeous." She pulled Brad to her, enjoying the feel of two men tight against her.

Paolo's hand eased to her skirt's zipper.

She tensed.

"It's okay." Brad released her.

"You don't have to if you don't want to," Paolo said.

"Of course I want to." Lizzie let the leather settee envelop her. She looked to the carpet rather than meet the men's eyes. "I think breaking up with the pig took my confidence."

"You need something stronger than coffee." Paolo tipped one brandy into another and pushed the double into her hands.

The first mouthful burned her throat, so her next sip was more cautious. She let the alcohol take her back to earlier, when Brad and Paolo had drowned her in flirts and gentle offers to fulfill her fantasy. *God, two hunks and a bathtub with no comeback. I'd be stupid not to,* she told herself. She took a third sip. "That's better. I'm more relaxed with a drink inside me." She put the glass down, stood, and reached to within a couple of inches of Brad's chest. "May I? It'll help get me back in the mood."

"Be my guest."

"Thank you. I guess this is where the party starts." Excitement had Lizzie quivering.

Brad gently took her shaking hand. "You're nervous."

"No, excited." Lizzie eased her hand free and flicked the shirt's middle button. With her other palm resting on Brad's shoulder and all the time looking into his sparkling blue eyes, she slipped her fingers inside his shirt. She first traced his firm pectoral, drawing a gasp as she teased a nipple on her way down, then slowly felt his iron-like six-pack, taking her time to enjoy every firm contour. She let the burgundy carpet warm and caresses her soles, enjoying the buzz the different touches on her hands and feet sent into her stomach. "God, this is a sexy room, and you're two gorgeous men."

"You're more than stunning yourself, Lizzie." Brad placed his hands around her waist, then lowered them to her hips, slowly, as if expecting her to object. His hold was as warm and reassuring as his smile. She took his hands and tucked them behind her back so he held her close.

Paolo's hands slid around her waist as well, enveloping her from behind to enclose her between both bodies. The Italian eased her hair aside and nuzzled the side of her neck. "Does this mean you're eager to go ahead?"

Lizzie moaned as butterflies dancing in her stomach gave the first hint of arousal. "God, yes."

"That's wonderful, my English Rose."

Brad nuzzled the other side of her neck, with his mop of hair and Paolo's stubble both tickling in different ways. Lizzie moaned in anticipation as Brad's eager fingers eased her skirt's zipper down, then loosened the button holding it in place. She almost felt two pairs of wet, soapy hands slipping over her flesh, arousing, caressing, and holding her in her decade-old fantasy. Butterflies of need in her stomach fluttered with vigor, threatening to head between her legs. *Please, not yet.* She nodded towards the bathroom. "Let's go in there."

With both men's arms around her, she led them toward the oak door. Her undone skirt threatened to slide over her hips until she grabbed its waistband, telling herself Brad could wait a few more minutes to find out what was beneath.

Paolo opened the door. His gentle hand on the small of her back invited Lizzie to enter first.

She gasped. The bathroom's warm burgundy paint matched the living room. The scent of aftershave was unmistakably Paolo. She wondered if the massive bath and the floor were marble and if the taps were gold. Even inside the bath, a row of lights was inlaid into the marble on each side, maybe a foot from the bottom. A discreet heater gave off warmth that, along with the decor and the brandy, enveloped and relaxed her. Above the bath, two flat bulbs in metal casings bolted to the ceiling gave off a low, sensual light. "God, this is even sexier than the living room." *What a place to get naked with these two.* She brushed her fingertips over one of the burgundy towels draped over a heated rail. It was soft and thick. "I'll look forward to wrapping this around me…you know, later."

"When we've finished," Brad said, "I hope to wrap it around you, if you'll let me."

Oooh…

Paolo's arm went back around her waist. His voice was low, his accent pure sex. "Only the best for my English Rose. We could put the bath in Jacuzzi mode, if you wish. There are scented soaps. We will do whatever it takes to indulge and relax you."

"Such gentlemen. Maybe a hug while we run the water," Lizzie suggested.

"Maybe a glass of champagne," Paolo suggested. "To celebrate your new life away from the pig."

"I'll never understand how anyone could treat someone as lovely as you so badly." Brad tutted.

"Thank you. Champagne would be good. We can celebrate one of you—hopefully—getting that promotion, too." Lizzie imagined sipping from a glass in the bath while Brad and Paolo slowly cleaned and aroused her... She shook away the thought. *In a few minutes. Take it easy. Relax. The anticipation will make it better.*

Paolo said, "I'll be back with a bottle and glasses in, as you English say, two ticks. If Bradley would run the water while I'm gone..."

"The pleasure will be all mine," Brad told the retreating figure, just before the door closed.

Lizzie watched the Australian's trousers tighten over his rear as he leaned over to push the faucet; one with a handle that bathers could use with their toes instead of having to sit up and twist with their hands. *I've always thought that decadent.* She sat on a stool. "The taps are gold, aren't they?"

"I think so. And those lights..." Brad pointed upward. "God knows how he can afford it. He's earning the same as me."

"His family is wealthy," Lizzie said.

"I didn't know they were that loaded. Each room must have cost thousands." Brad pushed his mop of hair aside.

God, he's sexy when he does that.

Paolo returned with a freshly opened champagne bottle and three glasses. He closed the door behind him. "May I pour you one, my English Rose?"

"Champagne and a posh bath with two studs fussing over me? Yes, please."

The Italian grinned. "It'll cost your skirt."

Lizzie gave a sigh of mock resignation. "I suppose it's a price worth paying." She stood, letting her mouth quirk into a smile while the Italian gave her a glass and poured. "Maybe I could swig champagne while Brad does the honors."

"It'll be a pleasure. After three years of wondering, I'll find out at last what lies beneath." Brad positioned himself behind her, with his hands holding the skirt. The butterflies in Lizzie's stomach fluttered with urgency as the Australian took control of the garment. *This is it.* Tension tightened her chest as he tugged it over her hips.

A noise in the living room. A floorboard creaked. *Footfall?* Lizzie grabbed her skirt as arousal drained. "What was that?"

Brad stilled. Paolo glanced from Lizzie to Brad with his mouth a straight line and his eyes flickering unease. He placed the champagne on the stool.

Brad stepped in front of Lizzie, protecting her while she fastened her skirt.

More footfalls, just beyond the door.

Paolo's wide brown eyes flitted from Brad to Lizzie then back to Brad, begging one of them to investigate.

Lizzie's throat was too locked to speak.

Knuckles tapped the door, firmly, with confidence.

Brad swallowed. "Who's there?"

Lizzie respected the lack of fear in his voice.

Another rap on the door.

Brad grabbed the door handle. He yelled, "Are you some sort of pervert come to watch?"

Lizzie noticed the cloud coming under the door a moment before Brad opened it, letting in a flood of the noxious, choking gas. She heard the men cough. The gas cloyed Lizzie's lungs and stung her eyes as it thickened, blotting out everything else. She dropped her glass so she could grab her throat, sending shards and champagne across the floor. She fell to her knees as she fought for breath, cutting palms and knees on broken glass, and crawled on her hands and knees. All she thought about was getting to the door, with the urge to survive greater than her fear of whoever waited outside.

Oh my God. Can't breathe.

Lizzie managed to crawl three or four feet before the world went black.

Chapter Two

Cold stone against her bare back. Headache. Pounding temples. Swimming mind.

Lizzie fought to open her eyes against the weakness and fatigue draining away too slowly.

Need to remember. I was with the boys. Smoke. Choking. Passed out. Her coughs only cleared her throat of some of the sting. Pain where broken glass had bit her palms and knees.

With her eyes still closed, she started to stretch taut muscles. Something pinned her on her back. *Can't move.* She groaned. *This isn't right. Oh my God. Need to focus.*

"Lizzie?" Paolo's voice, holding panic.

"Thank God. We thought…" Brad's voice.

Their tones had Lizzie quivering. She coughed again. Her tears took some sting from her eyes, so she opened them.

She wished her lids had stayed shut.

Paolo and Brad looked down at where she lay in the bath. Paolo's eyes were wide with terror, Brad's soft with concern. Clad only in underwear; Paolo in black briefs, Brad in tight grey shorts. Hands cuffed to the light fittings above their heads.

Oh my God. Lizzie blinked, long and slow, screwing her lids shut. *It will be different when I look again,* she assured herself.

She opened her eyes. Paolo and Brad still hung from the ceiling.

Lizzie started to sit up. She couldn't. She pushed and pulled and grunted but still couldn't move.

"It's okay, Lizzie," Brad said.

"No, it isn't okay," Paolo said.

With her mind clearing, Lizzie looked down her body, naked but for her light blue panties, at the metal bars pushed into the bath where the lights had been knocked out, pinning her beneath them. Paolo and Brad each stood on two bars with their hands chained above them. She tried to look over the bath's sides, but they were too high, and she could only see the men and the ceiling. Her fists clenched. "What's happening? Why are we like this? Who did it?"

"We don't know." Brad rattled his chains. "Paolo and I woke up hanging from the lights. We were worried you were dead."

"Let us out!" Paolo screamed. He pulled at his chains. "Who are you, you bastard? Pig! *Maiale!*" he spat.

"Let us out! Help!" Brad yelled.

Lizzie clenched her muscles. She tried to push the bars off her, but she couldn't move. Then she tried to maneuver her arms from her sides, but the bars pinned them, letting in the realization she'd been pushing away. *Oh my God, I'm trapped.* Her body first chilled, then trembled as fear and claustrophobia took hold. Finally, Lizzie screamed her panic. Then she sucked a breath and screamed again, and again, only stopping when her lungs were too painful to carry on. She thrashed, hitting the bars until she bruised herself.

The men yelled. Lizzie joined in when her lungs were ready.

Their screams were met by silence. Lizzie slumped, worn out and with her throat unable to shout any more. "Someone will have heard us."

Paolo bit a lip. He shook his head and looked away. *No.*

"This is a flat, for God's sake," Brad said. "You've got neighbors just the other side of the wall. They're only a few feet away."

"If we yell long enough, they'll complain about the noise," Lizzie said.

"No," Paolo said. "I like opera. I had the whole place sound-proofed so I could play it loud without anyone complaining."

"Oh, great." Lizzie's shoulders slumped.

"We need to do something soon," Brad said. "My wrists are getting sore."

"And hands above the head is fucking uncomfortable," Paolo said. "I can hardly feel my arms."

"Bang the walls," Lizzie suggested.

"We're too far from them. The only one near enough to reach is the outside one." Paolo looked down on Lizzie. "Can you do anything?"

"No. I'm pinned on my back." Fear gushed again, like a huge eruption coming from the pit of her stomach as visions of being left here to die, or someone coming in and stabbing her while she was defenseless, flowed through her. *Oh my God, oh my God, oh my God.* She forced herself to calm down in the hope thinking would distract her from the terror. "We need to work out what this is about. Who would do this, and why?"

"I've not got any enemies," Brad said.

Lizzie blew a stray strand of blonde hair from her mouth. "Nor me."

Paolo looked down, his eyes suddenly narrow, accusing her. "Your husband."

Lizzie thought. "No. He's a two-timing manipulative pig, but this isn't his style."

Brad and Lizzie looked at Paolo. Brad said, "Your family is wealthy. Getting rich makes you enemies."

"Like Lizzie, no one who would do this." The Italian's shrug made his chains rattle. He gritted his teeth and jerked downward, but his bonds stayed stubbornly chained to the light fitting. "Those builders did a great job of bolting everything. Too good a job."

Brad pulled downwards, too. Nothing moved. He winced and looked at his wrists, which were already red raw from the chaffing metal.

"By the Holy Mother, I'm not sure how much longer I can stay like this," Paolo said.

"Nor me. How are you doing?" Brad asked Lizzie.

"When I fantasized about being in a bathtub with you two, this wasn't what I imagined."

"My fantasy's not gone as planned, either." Brad nodded at Lizzie's lower half. "Light blue."

"Yeah."

"You look good in them."

"Ta," Lizzie said. "You two look great in yours as well."

Silence. Lizzie looked up at the two near-naked men whose bodies would have her squirming with desire under any other circumstances. She wondered if her flesh was doing as little for her colleagues. *Think about being trapped. Focus.* Twisting her neck under the upper-most bar let her look to her right at the steel bars wedged into the broken, sunken light fittings. She twisted to her left and saw the same.

"Can you see how they've fixed the bars?" Brad asked.

Lizzie shook her head.

"So, what do we do?" Paolo asked.

"We wait," Brad said.

"Is that it?" Paolo snapped.

"Unless you can think of anything better," Lizzie said, trying to keep her voice level. "Our best bet is probably you guys yanking at your chains and using your weight to rip them from the ceiling."

"You could try and pull your way out," Brad said.

"I've already tried, but I'll give it another go." Lizzie took a deep breath, trying to keep herself calm against the panic bubbling under the surface. She maneuvered her right hand so she could grab one of the steel bars. With a grunt of exertion, she tried to push herself along the bath, but friction had her back sticking to the marble. *My boobs probably wouldn't get under the bars anyway.*

She moved her left hand so she held a bar in both fists. With another grunt, she pushed upwards, straining every muscle, gritting her teeth, feeling sweat erupt.

The metal didn't give. She tried ramming it to the left, into the side of the bath, seeing if she could pull it from the light fitting. Nothing. She rammed it to the right, grunting with exertion until a bead of sweat trickled into her eye. Nothing. Her biceps ached from the effort, and she wished she could rub them. "Christ knows how they did this. It's not even moving."

"Okay, well done for trying," Brad said. "Relax. Keep your strength. You need to be slippy, with soap or something."

"The soap is in the sink," Paolo said. "I don't use it in the bath. I use gels and the like."

Lizzie ran her gaze along the bath's side and spotted a half-full, orange plastic bottle looking out of place amid the expensive decor. *Apricot Fresh,* the label said. Lizzie threw aside the unbidden thought that the Italian was more of a mint or lemon man. "Is that shampoo?"

"Bubble bath," Paolo said.

"Maybe you could tip it in. It'll be all slimy. That might help me move."

"Okay." Brad stepped onto the side of the bath, next to the bottle. His cuffs above the bath forced him to lean over and drew a wince as the steel rubbed against his already blood-raw wrists. His feet delicately tipped the bottle over and played with the top for a few seconds. "I'll never unscrew it with my toes." He stamped on the bottle, and again, and again. The plastic warped, and a tear appeared at the bottle's neck. Light orange fluid trickled into the bath, level with the small of Lizzie's back.

"A bit further this way. Get it under my shoulders, then with luck it'll slide down the slight slope," she told him.

Brad grunted his agreement. His toes shifted the bottle along, and he trod on it.

Lizzie watched a thick stream of orange fluid trickle down the bath's marble side, coming nearer until it was so close she had to cross her eyes to focus. Its fruity aroma was sweet, sickly, and strong, and too near her nose. Combined with the room's warmth and her stomach churning with fear, its smell had her fighting back vomit. *I can do without puking.* Moments later she felt its cool touch on her skin. She moved her shoulder up and down the couple of inches the bars allowed, feeling the bubble bath slick and slippery beneath her and letting it lubricate her against the marble.

Soon the bubble bath was slick across both her shoulders and back and clinging her panties to her rear and her hair to the marble, letting her slide from side to side if she pushed with her feet and palms. "Okay, here goes again." She clasped the steel rods in now-slick hands and managed to maneuver her soles against the bottommost rod. She pushed and pulled and felt her head against the bath's end.

"So far so good. You're doing great." With the bottle nearly empty, Brad stepped back into the bath with his feet on two rods, where he could stand straight. He gave his cuffs a yank, but the light fitting above didn't give.

Lizzie bent her neck, trying to force her body into a sitting position, fighting against the topmost bar keeping her on her back, battling the pain of trying to scrape her breasts beneath it, and of trying to bend her back more than was natural. "It's a bit easier with the bubble bath."

"You can do it," Brad said.

"Try harder," Paolo said.

"I am trying," Lizzie snapped. Fear and anger overrode the pain as she tried to contort her body through the narrow gap while trying to force her breasts beneath the bar. Even slick and slippery, the bar and the bath's shape let her go no further. She strained again, grunting with exertion. And again, and yet again. At last, after failing four times, she gave up and let herself slide back down the bath with tears streaming. "I'm sorry. I can't do it. I can't bend myself enough. I'll either scrape a boob off or break my back." She punched the marble in frustration, gaining some satisfaction from the pain. "Maybe in a while I'll be desperate enough."

"I think things are pretty desperate now." Paolo added a mutter in Italian.

"I tried my hardest," Lizzie repeated.

"You should try harder. Brad and I are relying on you."

Lizzie screamed her anger, a long, loud, wordless yell. "Of course I fucking tried," she snarled.

"Lizzie did her best. It's not her fault. She's as stuck as we are," Brad said.

"At least she's lying down. We're standing here with our wrists rubbed sore from these fucking cuffs."

"Maybe that's not as bad as being pinned on your back," Brad said.

"Yeah, don't judge lying here 'til you've tried it."

Paolo glared. "*Puttana*," was muttered, but clear.

"Don't you dare call me that," Lizzie snarled. "Only a while ago I was your English rose."

"Only because I wanted to fuck you. I didn't actually mean it."

"You bastard."

"Stop this!" Brad gave Lizzie a forced grin. "You'll always be my sheila."

Lizzie forced a smile in return. "Thanks, even if it doesn't sound as romantic."

"We don't argue. We need to stick together," Brad said.

"Stick together to do what?" Paolo asked. "I'm not just going to wait here to die."

"I don't know," Brad said.

"I'll try something then, seeing as your idea is only to stop arguing." Paolo grabbed the chain and lifted his feet from the rods. He hung suspended.

Lizzie bit a lip while she looked up at the light, searching and listening for a crack. *Please, come away.*

The fitting didn't budge. *Bugger.*

Paolo stood back down on the rods. He looked at the blood trickling from his wrists. "God, those chains cut into you when they're taking your weight."

"Tell me about it," Brad said.

"Someone will come in soon. We just have to wait," Lizzie said.

"What makes you so sure?" Paolo snapped.

"They're hardly likely to just leave us after being so imaginative putting us like this." Lizzie managed to keep her voice level. "Planning has gone into this."

"Maybe they're filming us. Waiting for us to die so they can sell the DVD." Paolo raised his voice to a scream. "You fucking perverts, making money out of us!"

The thought someone was enjoying her terror and watching her die chilled Lizzie.

"They won't just let leave us here," Brad said.

"Why not?" Paolo asked. "Are you an expert on snuff films?"

"We'll take ages to just die. Maybe a couple of days, I don't know. That's one hell of a boring film. *If* they're making a film, they'll want to come in and..." Brad shrugged. "You know, hurry things along."

"You mean, kill us quickly," Lizzie said.

Brad bit a lip. "No, not quickly. Entertainingly."

"Holy Mother." Paolo looked upwards and muttered in Italian. *A prayer,* Lizzie guessed.

She whimpered. "I think—"

The door opened.

Her head snapped to the sound, but Lizzie saw nothing over the bath's lip. Footfalls entered the bathroom, heavy boots slowly pacing the marble, deliberately, taking their time and drawing out the fear. The sound made her think of sadism and Nazi prison guards.

"Well, well, well," a woman's voice said.

"Jesus, we should have guessed. My day just got even worse," Brad said.

"You bitch," Paolo added. "*Puttana!*"

Lizzie strained her neck, but couldn't see over the rim. "Who is it?"

Approaching shoes beat the floorboards and Lizzie looked up into a face she recognized but couldn't place. Hazel eyes gazed down while the woman pushed her brown ponytail inside her combat top. Her mouth was a compassionless straight line.

Lizzie didn't like the baseball bat she held or the big knife sheathed in her leather belt.

"Aren't you all going to say hello?" the brunette asked.

"Cassandra, you cow," Paolo said. "Let us down."

Of course. Cassandra.

"What do you want?" Brad asked.

"We could start with the loan you gave me this morning. A hundred pounds." Cassandra tutted. "I wanted a thousand."

"We could get you a thousand," Brad said.

"You didn't want to give me anything earlier, Bradley. At least Paolo arranged a hundred for me."

"Cut us down, and we'll arrange it, no questions asked," Brad said.

"One of you might arrange it while the other phones the police."

"We wouldn't," Paolo said. "I promise. Please, just let us down."

"I'll think about it." Lizzie heard Cassandra's long, slow footfall pace the bathroom beyond her vision. Knowing who did this didn't make Lizzie feel better.

After what seemed like minutes, but Lizzie supposed could only have been a few seconds, Cassandra returned to the bathtub. She stared at Paolo.

The Italian's tears landed on Lizzie's thigh.

"Or, instead of Bradley's meanness with the bank's money, we could make the issue that Paolo smothers a girl in compliments, fucks her, and then walks away, leaving her to take the rap." The baseball bat slowly, gently, caressed Paolo's face like a lover's fingertips tracing his contours as he hung his head. Paolo's next tear tangled in his stubble. The bat found the underside of his chin and lifted his head so Cassandra could stare into his face. She ran her fingertips over Paolo's ribs, cooing as she found his six-pack. "If you live through tonight, Elizabeth, you'll soon understand exactly what I mean."

Lizzie regarded the woman. *Thirty, maybe. Brown hair, hazel eyes. Decent looking. Cute ponytail. Not a stereotypical psychopath.*

Cassandra ran her fingertips down Paolo's flesh, reaching the waist-band of his briefs. He jerked back, making his chains rattle and the metal rods bow and press into Lizzie's thighs.

"And Bradley is a pig, too, of course." Cassandra reached into a pock-et and pulled out a phone.

"That's mine!" Brad said.

"Shall we see who's been leaving messages for you, wondering where you are?" Cassandra asked.

Brad bit a lip. He flushed as he looked from Paolo to Lizzie, then away.

Cassandra laughed. She tossed the phone onto the stool.

Lizzie grimaced as she imagined the baseball bat pounding her de-fenseless face into a mask of blood with a broken nose and teeth and her skull crushed, unable to fight back or protect herself. She drew a deep breath. "What about me?"

The brunette cocked her head to look down with hard, unyielding eyes. "What about you?"

Lizzie stared back, refusing to look away.

"What are you doing here, Elizabeth?" Cassandra gave a mock frown. "It is Elizabeth, isn't it?"

Lizzie nodded.

"Lizzie hasn't done anything to upset you. You need to let her go," Brad said.

Snarling, Cassandra swung the bat. It slammed Brad's thigh with a soft thud. "I don't think you're in any position to make demands, Bradley." She let the bat beat a slow rhythm on her free palm while looking back down at Lizzie. "I asked what you are doing here, in a bathroom with two men and your skirt falling off before I intervened. And when I ask a question, I get very impatient if I don't get a reply." The bat beat its rhythm.

Silence. Lizzie looked to Paolo. He turned away, lost his balance on the rods, and his foot landed on her thigh. Lizzie yelped as pain seared.

"Sorry," Paolo muttered. He balanced back on the iron rods.

Lizzie looked at Brad. He shrugged.

The bat beat its rhythm quicker, impatiently. "Could you have come here for sex, Elizabeth?" Cassandra's tone carried mock shock.

The bat beat its rhythm. "Well? Someone answer."

Silence.

Cassandra swung the bat, hitting Paolo's kneecap with a wet squelch. The Italian gasped, biting his lip and throwing his head back.

"I asked if Elizabeth came here for sex. If I don't get an answer, I'll smash Bradley's knee. Is that clear?"

"We've had a night out." Brad peered at Cassandra through the blond mop now plastered to his face by sweat. "We've all had a bit to drink, and coming back here seemed like fun."

"Sex." Cassandra said the word as if it had crawled up her nose and left a foul smell.

"I suppose it might have been heading that way," Paolo said.

"When you said you wondered what she wears underneath, I thought it was headed that way, too," Cassandra said.

"You spied on us," Brad said.

"If that's what you want to call it. Anyway, does her underwear disappoint?"

"No. Lizzie looks great," Brad said.

Paolo's groan broke the silence. He bent then straightened his bruising knee.

"Are you going to let us out?" Lizzie asked.

Cassandra cocked her head to stare back with no expression in her features, as if knowing not speaking had extra fear squirming in Lizzie's stomach.

"You have to tell us," Brad said.

"I don't think I have to do anything I don't want to." Snarling, Cassandra swung the bat. The Australian jerked around, making it only a glancing blow to the knee. "Do I?"

"No," Brad said.

"But maybe I will tell you, anyway. Would you like that?"

Silence.

The bat beat a rhythm on her palm. "I asked if you would like that."

"Yes, please." Lizzie's words came out as a hoarse whisper.

"Okay, as you asked politely, I'll tell you."

Chapter Three

Cassandra disappeared from view. Lizzie heard footfalls on the marble, slow, rhythmic, and malevolent enough to have her shivering.

Unable to see their tormentor, Lizzie watched Brad and Paolo instead. Brad's eyes showed something between hate and anger, Paolo's displayed fear and let occasional tears slide into his stubble.

Cassandra still paced too slowly. The bat beat its rhythm.

Tell us. Please tell us, Lizzie begged silently. Terror had her gripping the bar in hands slickened by bubble bath and terror-induced sweat.

"It's the betrayal, you see," Casandra said suddenly. "Bradley giving out loans left, right and center, to everyone except me."

"I explained, you've got a record of not repaying," Brad said.

Brad yelped as the bat slammed his kneecap. He threw his head back with his face screwed, as if trying not to show pain.

Cassandra peered over the bath. The hazel eyes looking down on Lizzie were deep pools. "You seem to know these *men...*" The last word was almost spat. "…quite well."

Lizzie silently begged the bat not to slam into her face. "I've worked with them for a couple of years."

"I'm sure you'll agree the world isn't big enough for both their egos." The hazel glare demanded agreement.

Lizzie's stomach turned to liquid.

"I said, the world isn't big enough for these two egos. An answer would be polite, Elizabeth."

"Yes."

"I thought you'd agree." Cassandra flicked open the sheath at her belt and brought out a hunting knife. The blade flickered in the artificial light as she looked down on it, examining it as if it was expensive jewelry.

Lizzie blinked. *Oh my God, she's going to cut us to bits.*

Paolo whimpered. Brad's swallow was audible.

Cassandra slowly looked from the blade to Lizzie. "So, my dear, the world is only big enough for one of these pigs, and you know both of them well. Which is less vile?"

Lizzie blinked.

Cassandra ran a forefinger slowly, almost sensually, along the blade's edge, drawing blood that stained the steel and dripped onto the marble. She licked her finger, leaving a scarlet smear on her lip. "Seeing as how you chose not to answer that question, Elizabeth, I'll ask a different one I hope you'll find a little easier. Which of these two *gentlemen* shall I kill."

Lizzie blinked again. *Oh My God, oh my God, oh my God.* The question swirled in her mind but refused to form.

Brad suddenly yelled. He kicked, swiping his foot at the fist clasped around the knife. He kicked again, and again, yelling and screaming and swearing. "Let us go, you bitch. You're fucking crazy."

The knife clattered on the marble. Cassandra leaped back, away from Brad's bare feet and out of Lizzie's sight.

Cassandra lurched back into view with her eyes blazing and teeth clenched. The bat pounded Brad's hip. He yelped. The bat swung again and again, catching the Australian's defenseless body half a dozen times until blood trickled from a weal on his thigh and bruises started to form. His head hung limp.

Cassandra looked down on Lizzie with her eyes suddenly soft again. "These two really are pigs, aren't they, my dear?"

Lizzie didn't reply.

"Ah, the strong silent type. Anyway, as I was saying, the world isn't big enough for both their egos. Which pig shall we cull?"

Lizzie whimpered. Her gaze flicked from man to man, then back at Cassandra. Brad's eyes were soft, Paolo's begging, and Casandra's wide hazel orbs questioning, with the bat beating its rhythm on her palm. The knife was back in its sheath.

"Don't kill us," Paolo begged. "Please."

"We'll give you the loan," Brad said. "Come in tomorrow, and we'll have the papers waiting for you. Discretionary minimum interest."

Cassandra cocked her head. "So, I've suddenly become low risk, have I?"

Brad hung his head.

"I thought not." Cassandra looked at Lizzie. "Which one shall we kill?"

Lizzie squirmed under those dark eyes. Jumbling thoughts numbed her mind.

"Lizzie won't choose between us," Paolo said.

"I think she will," Cassandra said.

"I can't." Lizzie sobbed. *Oh my God, oh my God, oh my God.* "Please don't make me choose."

"Why not?" Cassandra asked with forced innocence, as if she indulged a five-year-old.

"I just can't," Lizzie said.

"Hmmm. I think I might have to encourage you." Cassandra turned the hot tap.

Boiling water. Searing heat. Agony. Lizzie screamed. *Oh my God.* She jerked against the rods. They wouldn't give. She screamed again. Fought the rods. *Oh my God.* Boiling and scalding.

Cassandra slammed the cold tap, then turned off both taps and pulled the plug's handle. The water drained, leaving steam and Lizzie quivering with shock. Cassandra replaced the plug. "There. I think you will make a decision, Elizabeth, or I'll turn the tap back on and leave it running. I'm not sure whether you'd scald to death first or drown as the boiling water rises, but I'm sure it would be unpleasant whichever order it happens in.

"You cow," Brad said.

Lizzie's body slumped. With the bubble bath and water slick against her back, she slid down the marble a little.

"So, you see, Elizabeth," Casandra said, "you will decide for me."

Lizzie's eyes welled as she looked form Brad to Paolo. "I don't know."

"Maybe, when I've told you a little story about each of your friends, you'll be a bit more inclined to make a decision." Cassandra laughed.

"I don't think Lizzie wants to hear any stories," Paolo said.

He's right. I'm not in the mood. Lizzie sobbed.

"Elizabeth might like to know how you both line your own pockets at her expense."

Paolo looked at Lizzie, then flicked his gaze away.

Lizzie frowned. *What has he got to hide?*

"I see you're interested in hearing about Paolo, my dear," Cassandra said. "Then we can talk about Bradley."

Brad lifted his head. "Me?"

"Yes, you. Has he promised you anything, Elizabeth?"

"Like what?" Lizzie asked.

"Like promising tonight will be special, and that he'll always remember it, and that you'll always be friends?"

Lizzie looked up at the Australian. "Something like that."

He shrugged.

"And like, when you and he went for that promotion, a couple of years ago…"

"He got that fair and square," Lizzie said. "It was just him and me."

The stool scraped over the marble, and seconds later Cassandra sat at the bath's head end, well away from any kick the men might aim. She looked down at Lizzie, first meeting her gaze, then slowly glancing down Lizzie's body. She licked her lips. "You know, Elizabeth, if things were different, I could quite fancy you."

Lizzie covered her breasts with her hands as best she could.

"You're a pretty girl, and you're just lying there, defenseless. I'm tempted to take advantage."

Oh my God, please, no. Lizzie clamped her legs together, tried harder to cover her breasts.

Cassandra licked her lips. "I do like a girl looking nervous to terrified. Yes, like that, with tears being squeezed out. And the way you're shaking is a real turn on."

"Leave her alone," Brad said.

Cassandra's head shot up. "That's very loyal of you, Bradley, although I should let my bat hurt you for your outburst. But wouldn't you like to watch me give Elizabeth the time of her life?"

Oh my God no. "Please, no."

"No, Elizabeth? Don't you want to make love to me with these two men watching? Personally, I'd find it a turn on, and I'm surprised you're turning me down. We've already established you're here for sex, you disgusting slut."

Lizzie shook her head, unable to force out words.

"Bradley seems desperate to maintain your dignity. I'll tell you what, Bradley, I won't force myself on Lizzie if you and Paolo let my bat pound you."

The men looked at each other.

Take the beatings, you bastards, Lizzie begged silently.

Cassandra gave a mock sweet grin. "I like my sex rough. Maybe inflicting a bit of pain, if you know what I mean."

"Please, no," Lizzie begged again.

"We'll take the beatings," Brad said.

Paolo glared.

"Paolo?" Cassandra asked.

After a short pause, he nodded.

"Good." Cassandra grabbed the bat. She swung.

Paolo yelped as the bat slammed into his undefended stomach. He gagged.

Please, don't puke over me.

The bat pounded Brad's ribs now. Lizzie wondered if she heard a bone crack or whether it was just the bat hitting his body.

"Thank you," Lizzie told her colleagues. Both were too busy groaning to acknowledge.

"That was fun, but I think I'd have preferred the sex. You look so gorgeous, lying there naked and vulnerable." Cassandra sighed. "I guess you're more interested in these pigs. Maybe when we've had our chat you'll feel differently and you'll be more inclined to let me cull one."

Lizzie looked from Paolo to Brad. Paolo looked away from her gaze. Brad shrugged. The bruise on his chest already formed. Both hung limp. She asked, "Are either of you going to tell me what the hell Cassandra is talking about."

"Whatever she says, she's lying, *amore.*" Paolo still didn't look at her.

"Only a few minutes ago she was a bitch." Cassandra unsheathed the knife.

The Italian stilled as she gently touched his knee with the blade, then slowly traced it up his thigh, all the time moving slowly inside his leg. "Before we puncture your manhood, would you clarify, is Elizabeth your *amore* or a bitch?"

"*Amore*," he whispered, still looking at the wall.

Cassandra continued to move the knife, only stopping when the point rested on his briefs' bulge.

Paolo stiffened.

Please don't stab him, Lizzie begged silently. *Not there.*

"Say it louder, Paolo," Cassandra ordered.

"*Amore.*"

"Look at her and say it."

Paolo looked at the wall. Tears ran down his face.

"Do it!" The knife prodded.

Paolo screamed. His chains rattled as he hung limp.

"For God's sake, you cowardly pig, that was only a nip. If you don't do as I say, I'll really give you something to complain about," Cassandra said.

The Italian looked down. A tear landed on Lizzie's stomach. "*Amore.*"

Cassandra withdrew the knife. "Good boy. That wasn't too difficult, was it? Now, will you tell Elizabeth how you treat your *amore*, or shall I?"

Paolo looked away.

Cassandra gave a long, deep sigh. "So, it's down to me to spill the beans. Paolo and I have a financial arrangement."

"Your finances aren't my business." With a sob, Lizzie gave the rods another despairing push. They didn't move. "Please, just let me go."

Cassandra nestled on the stool, as if ready to tell a long story. "Our finances *are* your business, Elizabeth, because they'll send you to prison while I'm leading the good life." She looked up at Paolo. "He's making money, too."

Paolo looked away. His, "Don't listen," didn't convince Lizzie, even when she told herself he'd just taken a beating for her.

"Do you remember six months ago, Elizabeth, the bollocking you got for giving me ten thousand rather than a single thousand?"

"I went over and over it in my mind. I'm sure I only input three noughts."

"You did, Elizabeth. Your friend Paolo put in the extra after logging on using your ID." Cassandra glanced around the bathroom. "It looks as if his share went on décor."

Lizzie's stomach chilled. "Is this true, Paolo?"

The way the Italian looked away, biting his lip, gave Lizzie her answer.

"You bastard," she snarled. "And I suppose that hundred you authorized today…"

"Yes, Elizabeth. A couple of extra zeros under your ID. We'd keep going until you were sacked or prosecuted, but now you're leaving, Paolo has ended our arrangement." Cassandra pulled the knife. "I'm not happy about that and came here tonight to end it permanently. It's a wonderful bonus to find my accomplice has company."

Lizzie covered her chest again, not wanting to give Paolo a view. *The pig.*

Cassandra stood. She caressed the hunting knife before running the flat of the blade across Paolo's stomach. "Now do you see why I thought you might want him killed? He is happy to send you to jail to line his pockets."

"You bastard," Lizzie snarled.

"Do you want him killed?" Cassandra asked.

"If we ever get out of here, I'll make him sorry."

Paolo looked away.

"Not that it leaves Bradley in the clear, of course."

"It can't be as bad as what Paolo's done," Lizzie said

Cassandra gave a low, long laugh. She looked at the Australian. "Would you like to enlighten Elizabeth, or shall I?"

"Brad?" Lizzie asked. *Not Brad, please. He's so nice.*

He looked away.

"So, you've gone all silent, have you?" Cassandra lifted Brad's phone. "Shall we see who's leaving messages?"

Brad kicked out but was too far away and missed the fist holding the phone. He yelled, kicking again, but Cassandra had already lurched away. Brad winced, looking up at his wrists, now red raw with blood smearing his bonds.

Cassandra grasped the bat in both hands.

"Please don't," Lizzie begged.

"He deserves it," the brunette snarled.

"I don't care. I don't want him hurt," Lizzie said.

Cassandra sat. "Maybe you'll be a little less sympathetic when you realize he's screwed you out of thousands of pounds."

Lizzie looked up. Brad briefly met her gaze, then looked away. "What did you do, Brad?"

He didn't speak.

"As he's gone all quiet, I suppose I'll have to tell you," Cassandra said. "Do you know Becky Malone?"

Brad moaned.

Lizzie tried to think. The name was familiar.

"She interviewed us today," Paolo said.

Lizzie remembered. "That's right. She was on the interview panel when Brad and I went for his job."

"Cute," Cassandra said. "High flier. Red hair, green eyes, gorgeous. Isn't that right, Bradley?"

"I'd not noticed."

"Liar." Cassandra swung the bat. It caught Brad's thigh with a slap. He threw his head back and groaned.

"What's she got to do with you?" Lizzie asked Cassandra.

"That's a good question, Elizabeth, and it has a simple answer." Cassandra paced the marble, slow and steady, with the bat slapping a beat on her palm.

So, if the answer is simple, tell me.

Cassandra paced. The bat slapped her palm.

Desperation, a need to know, screwed Lizzie's stomach. She banged at the bars while grunting her frustration and just about held back a yell. She ached to leap from the bath, to pound the information from the brunette.

"Do I sense a little frustration, Elizabeth?"

"Just tell us."

"Becky is my cousin," Cassandra said. "We talk all the time."

"Shit," Bradley muttered.

"I never told her of my little financial arrangement with Paolo, of course. But she knows all about Bradley."

Lizzie looked up.

"She's very fond of Bradley. She would do anything for him." Cassandra jabbed a button the phone, calling up Brad's voicemail.

"Brad? It's gone ten. Where are you? You promised me, if I gave you the job, you'd be here..."

Paolo swung around to kick his colleague. "You're fucking her so she'll give you the job instead of me. Pig! *Maiale!*"

Brad lurched from another kick. He screeched as his bonds bit, and Lizzie saw the broken skin flapping where the steel cut.

"Bastardo!" Paolo screamed as he kicked again, catching the Australian's calf.

Brad winced.

"Excellent! You're saving me from having to hit him myself." Cassandra looked down at Lizzie. "Of course, Becky already had her claws into Brad when she interviewed you both that time. She told me you were the better candidate, but she couldn't resist Bradley's body. And that's why he was looking at his watch earlier—he had a promotion to confirm in my cousin's bed." She looked at the Australian, then ran her fingertips over his muscles. "And in fairness, I can see why Becky wants him."

Brad spat. "Bitch."

Cassandra wiped the phlegm from her cheek, then examined her wet fingers. She grabbed the bat. "I don't like being spat at, Bradley."

The Australian screamed as the bat pounded him, on the thighs, his knee, his rump and stomach, then his ribs. He jerked, releasing more blood from his wrist.

He was still screaming when Cassandra placed the bat on the stool and looked back down at Lizzie. "That was two years ago. How much was the pay raise with promotion? Two, three thousand a year?"

"Probably. I can't think straight enough to process numbers."

"So, Elizabeth, these two pigs have both shafted you good and proper. And only earlier this evening you couldn't wait to get in this very bath with them both." She patted the marble.

Lizzie looked from man to man. Paolo stared at the wall, Brad held the chain, keeping it from rubbing his wrists. He bit a lip and looked down at the bath's far end, like a schoolboy scolded by a teacher.

Lizzie knew hatred twisted her features, for the men who had let her down, and for the woman who pinned her here. "Bastards," she muttered.

"I know," Cassandra said. "So, to ensure your own freedom, which of these pigs shall I kill?"

Lizzie stared through unfocusing eyes. Her heart thumped her ribs.

"Brad's a loser. He has to sleep around to get a promotion." Paolo looked down at Lizzie. "Choose him."

The Australian swung his bare foot, catching Paolo on the knee Cassandra's bat had already pounded. "You cowardly bastard. You've got a dickey heart. You could pop off at any time, anyway."

"Brad! Stop! Just stop!" Lizzie yelled.

Brad kicked again.

"Brad!" Lizzie screamed.

"So, Elizabeth, you nominate Bradley," Cassandra said.

The Australian's head jerked to Cassandra.

Paolo's cheeks puffed out.

"No. I didn't nominate anyone," Lizzie shouted. *Oh my God, oh my God, oh my God.*

"Don't lie, Elizabeth. I heard you say his name. In fact, you shouted it twice." Cassandra pulled her knife, slowly, drawing out the moment.

Lizzie's gaze fixed on the blade, about six inches long and with newly polished steel glinting.

"I expect you're really sorry you refused all my loan requests, now, aren't you, Bradley?" Cassandra asked.

Brad stared at the knife. A fleck of spittle appeared on his bottom lip as he whimpered, to become a long strand of dribble. Lizzie hardly noticed it land on her belly.

Cassandra eased the blade nearer the Australian, with the baseball bat clenched in her other fist. She moved slowly and gracefully, as if having trouble pushing the blade through the atmosphere Lizzie felt thicken by the second.

The blade rested against Brad's quivering six-pack. Cassandra said, "If any of you so much as move a muscle, I'll push this in. Do you all understand?"

Silence.

Cassandra twisted the knife. Brad moaned as a pinprick of blood trickled down his stomach to stain his shorts. "I asked if you all understood."

Paolo and Lizzie murmured. Brad whimpered.

Cassandra placed the bat on the bath's side and wiped the blood from Brad's stomach with her free hand. She shuddered and gave a light moan while inspecting her slick fingers, then licked her lips as she traced her hand over Brad's stomach. "You've got a lovely six-pack, Bradley," Cassandra purred as she smeared the blood. More claret trickled from the puncture, and her fingertips spread it over his chest. She cooed as she caressed his pectorals. "Your body is even better with blood. Lovely, just lovely."

Brad gurgled.

Lizzie watched, transfixed by terror; sweat erupted, sheening her flesh, and she was unable to unlock her breath. A drop of blood landed on her stomach. *Ugh.* She wanted to scream but could only watch in horrified fascination as the brunette's scarlet fingertips traced Brad's contours.

"You can stop now, Casandra," Paolo said. "You've made your point. You've scared us shitless. We're all sorry."

Cassandra cocked her head. "Are you really all sorry?"

"Yes," the three said.

Cassandra's two brown pools gazed down. Lizzie tried to look away but found her eyes drawn to the brunette's. "What exactly are you sorry for, Elizabeth?" Cassandra asked.

Lizzie's pounding temples stopped her thinking clearly. Another drop of Brad's blood had her recoiling in distaste, the action hurting as the bar across her hips dug in. "You told me I was in trouble for coming here with two men," she said.

"Yes. You're under the rods because you're a disgusting slut." Cassandra shook her head in mock sadness. "Fancy having a threesome with these two pigs."

"I'm sorry. Please, let me go."

Cassandra paused, as if knowing taking her time increased Lizzie's terror. "Maybe I could just turn on the hot tap. Full power." She grabbed the handle.

Lizzie squealed. "No. Please don't. I'll do anything."

Cassandra's smile twisted. "I'll think about it. Maybe I'll turn the tap, maybe I won't. But first, back to the matter in hand. Bradley."

Lizzie cursed herself for being relieved the attention went to someone else.

"How shall I kill you, Bradley?" The brunette cocked her head, raised the knife and held it in her left fist, then her right, and laughed as Brad's head followed the motion. "You are funny, Bradley." She slowly moved the knife in a wide arc above her head. Brad's eyes followed before she eventually rested the blade just above his right hip.

Brad's shudder jangled his chain. "Please don't."

"Aah, I do love it when men beg," Cassandra said.

Another scarlet drop landed on Lizzie's stomach. *Ugh.*

"The risk is a turn on, isn't it?" Casandra ran the blade gently over Brad's flesh. "I might sneeze. One of you might attack me. Anything could make the knife slip and puncture you. It might slide in all the way to the hilt." She licked her lips and looked from the blade to his face. "That would be awful, wouldn't it?"

Brad's mouth hung open.

Paolo clenched eyes, squeezing out tears. Lizzie's gaze fixed on the knife.

"I think we'll stop playing now," Cassandra said. "Would you all like that?"

Silence.

Cassandra prodded Brad's stomach with the blade's tip. A new glob of blood appeared.

The Australian jerked away.

"Come back here, or I'll slice you," Cassandra snarled.

Chewing a lip, Brad straightened himself.

Without warning, Cassandra slashed his stomach. And again.

Chapter Four

Screaming. Blood pouring. *Oh my God.* Lizzie shut her eyes but couldn't keep out the slick dampness. *Blood splashing me.* Cassandra's adrenaline-fuelled yell. Paolo groaned.

Something slopped on Lizzie's stomach. *What was that?* She decided she didn't want to know. *Oh my God.* Brad's feet landed on her thighs. Smell of blood.

Cassandra applauded. Her squeal was one of delight.

The need to know outweighed the fear and revulsion. Lizzie slid an eye open.

Blood. Everywhere. Covering Lizzie, filling the bath.

Brad hung limp, jerking, his lower half a mass of blood and his tummy hanging open. He moaned.

Cassandra squealed.

Lizzie gagged.

Paolo's vomit splattered the heap of Brad's intestines lying on Lizzie's stomach.

Lizzie gagged again. Panic. Screamed. Shoved at the rods. Tried to push her way out. She failed.

Cassandra laughed through the scarlet splatters on her front. "You're all so entertaining!"

Brad hung limply from his chains with his chin on his chest.

Lizzie screamed. *Oh my God, Brad is dead.* She screamed again. *Oh my God, I'm covered in gore. Oh my God, oh my God, oh my God.* The intestines slid slickly and slowly off her stomach. The long, pink bloodied length fell beside her in the bath, mingling with blood and vomit.

Lizzie screamed.

A final length fell from Brad's gash, landing with a squelch on her stomach to coil like an obscene snake.

Lizzie screamed.

Paolo groaned. His body was splattered with Brad's blood.

"Splendid!" Casandra reached for the open champagne bottle and filled a glass. The stem was immediately slick within her bloodied fingers as she raised the glass in a toast and drank.

Paolo whimpered. "Please, let me go."

Cassandra cocked her head to regard the Italian. She sipped more champagne. "I suppose I did tell Lizzie I would only kill one of you."

"Please," Paolo said.

Please, Lizzie thought, too, from her bath of blood, intestines, and vomit. *How can you calmly drink champagne when you've slaughtered Brad?* She quietly shoved at a bar, more in desperation than expectation.

Brad's stomach dripped more blood over her torso and matted her hair.

"My car is outside," Cassandra said. "Stolen of course, so there's no trace. Even if I let you go, by the time the alarm is raised, I'll be in my safe house."

Lizzie heard the brunette drag the stool across the floor, then saw her stand on it next to Paolo. "You won't try anything silly while I unscrew your chains, will you?" she asked the Italian, tapping the bloodied hilt at her belt. "I wouldn't want to have to use my friend here," she said in a tone suggesting she ached to use the knife.

Paolo gurgled.

"I asked if you will try anything if I unscrew your cuffs."

"He won't," Lizzie said. "Just let us go."

"Patience, patience, Elizabeth."

"I'm stuck here in a bath of blood. Please let me go." Lizzie swallowed back bile. She felt the blood caking on her, almost crawling over her as it trickled, as if it was a living thing.

"I suppose I see your point. I'd probably be a tad impatient in your position. I'm sure when Paolo is free he'll arrange your release." Cassandra pulled a screwdriver from her combat trousers and worked on the light fitting Paolo hung from.

The Italian looked up with wide eyes, and for the first time, Lizzie saw hope in his features.

Cassandra cursed as the screwdriver slipped from her slick fingers, but she caught it before it fell to the marble. She gave a grunt of satisfaction when one of the three screws came away and clattered to the floor, then another, leaving the fitting hanging by only one screw. Lizzie hoped

Paolo would easily tug it away.

Cassandra slapped the Italian's cheek. "You can pull yourself free. It'll take you a minute or two, and believe me, I'll be well gone. I hope you'll think of me when you're mentally scarred by this." She glanced down at Lizzie. "I actually like you, Elizabeth. I'm sorry you ended up getting covered in Bradley's insides, genuinely I am."

"So am I."

"Under different circumstances, I think we could have been friends," Cassandra said.

I doubt it.

Without another glance to either Paolo or Lizzie, Cassandra strode from the bathtub. Lizzie heard footfalls cross the marble, then the bathroom door close. She couldn't stop thinking of claret footprints staining Paolo's expensive living room carpet.

Paolo's head hung. He gasped. His face went scarlet.

The front door closed. *She's gone.* Lizzie looked up at the Italian. "Get us out," she forced between sobs. She glanced at Brad's bloodied corpse with the scarlet gash across his stomach, smelled the aromas of blood and vomit. "I said, get us out. Quick. I can't stand this."

Paolo jerked, rattling his chains. He gasped. Jerked again. Gasped for breath. Jerked. Gasped. Purple face.

Oh my God, heart attack. Oh my God.

Paolo sucked a deep, wheezed breath before giving one more violent jerk, then slumped. His feet left the bars to collapse on Lizzie's stomach, winding her.

The room fell quiet. No crying or pleading for mercy, no jangling of chains. The silence had Lizzie forcing herself to calm against another tide of panic. "Paolo?" she asked, cautiously. *Please, answer.*

Paolo's chains creaked into the quiet.

"Paolo!" Lizzie shouted. *Oh my God, he's dead. Oh my God, oh my God.* She screamed as panic enveloped her like a shroud. She kicked and thrashed in the bath of blood and guts and vomit as much as she could with the bars pinning her.

Her effort only succeeded in covering her with more blood, matting her hair, gluing her eyelids together, tasting it in her mouth.

She stilled.

Be calm. Think your way out of this. Paolo and Brad won't arrive at work. Someone will look for them.

In a day or two, maybe. Oh my God.

Lizzie wept as she imagined lying trapped for days in the bath with two bodies hanging above her, forced to survive by drinking congealing blood mingled with vomit and her excrement; flies filling the room to buzz over the rotting corpses and laying eggs on her; the stench as the men started to decay.

Lizzie slammed her lids shut rather than look at the blood and death.

Something cracked. Lizzie's eyes jerked open to see the light fitting holding Paolo up bend a little.

Only one screw.

The chain creaked. She prayed, hoped the body wouldn't land on her head.

Then she hoped he didn't land where his sightless eyes would stare at her until they decomposed, with insects crawling over his sockets and into his nostrils.

The fitting finally snapped. Paolo dropped like a stone, flopping onto the taps. His chains caught in the faucet, turning the tap on.

Lizzie screamed as scalding water streamed into the bloodied bath.

ABOUT THE AUTHORS

W.C. Jones first started writing in the eighth grade after an addiction to R.L. Stine's *Fear Street* and many collections of horror stories by such masters of the craft as Edgar Allan Poe, Nathaniel Hawthorne, Shirley Jackson, and Stephen King. He has been published in several venues over the past few years including *Allegory, Horrorbites,* and *9Terrors.* He takes inspiration through all mediums including music, video games, and everyday life. He currently lives in Beebe, AR, with his wife and son, along with a black cat named Poe, who constantly finds a way to sleep on his shoulders.

A resident of North Carolina's Outer Banks, **A.P. Sessler** frequents an alternate universe not too different from your own, searching for that unique element that twists the everyday commonplace into the weird. When he's not writing fiction, he composes music, makes art, and spends too much time trying to connect with his inner genius. He also likes to dress in funny clothes and talk about the first English colony in the New World.

Andrew Richardson lives in Wiltshire, England, with his wife, a rescue cat, and a son who occasionally pops in. He is within easy reach of Stonehenge and other historical places whose regal solitude provides a clear mind for working out plot difficulties and story ideas. Most of his work falls squarely into the horror or 'historical fantasy' genres, although he occasionally switches to erotica so his characters can have some fun for a change!

Andrew dislikes laptops so adopts the old and quaint approach of typing with a desktop, which at least has a screen big enough to avoid the need to squint.

Andrew has a background in history and archaeology and has worked in several trenches. When he's not writing or working Andrew follows Aldershot Town Football Club and takes long walks over rugged countryside

Press
Presents

Grave Markers, Volume Four
(includes Joseph Rubas's *The Freaks Come Out at Night*, A.P. Sessler's *The First Suitor*, and Neil Davies's *Vampire Worms*)

Grave Markers, Volume Three
(includes Dominic Stabile's *Full Moon in the West*, Adrian Ludens's *Bottled Spirits*, and S.L. Williams's *The Dance*)

Grave Markers, Volume Two
(includes Hal Badner's *Tolerance*, Sebastian Bendix's *Shriek of the Harpy*, and Russell Coy's *The One Who Lies Next to You*)

Grave Markers, Volume One
(includes Richard Black's *Nikolis Cole: the Low-Rise Saint*, Sebastian Bendix's *Rock, Paper, Scissors*, and Joshua Rex's *Coattails*)

www.ingramcontent.com/pod-product-compliance
Lightning Source LLC
Chambersburg PA
CBHW070828180626
46818CB00001B/434